Between Once & Forever

Volume One

written & illustrated by
Jonathan Hawker

line & copy edits by
Alex Johnson

Copyright © 2024 by Majesty Publications, LLC

All rights reserved.

No portion of this book may be reproduced in any form without written permission from the publisher or author, except as permitted by U.S. copyright law.

Dearest Traveler, thank you for joining me for these joyous moments in Aaron and Morgan's lives.

The Between Once & Forever collection is full of cozy, swoony and spicy moments that our heroes have shared, whether in Etna City or long ago, in Camelot...

While mostly comfy and sweet, this is still Etna, so please be cautious of your mental health for some brief moments within.

Content warnings include, but are not limited to: explicit language, consumption of alcohol, consumption of tobacco, mention of recreational drugs, murder, death, blood, and violence.

Sweet indeed, a reconciliation comprised of intimate touches and first times.

We begin with a tale you may be familiar with—the very night Arthur came to Morgan's bedroom after a stolen kiss woke something inside him, forcing him to come to terms with what his heart desired.

This was the first on page spice I ever attempted. As Awakening in Sapphire had already been finalized, it became the bonus scene at the end.

Sapphire now contains its proper open door moment between Morgan and Aaron, and so this scene has a new home within these pages.

This scene was released on April 19th, 2024 in the first edition of Awakening in Sapphire

His Sweet Boy

Camelot - The Reign of His Majesty, Uther Pendragon

Without undressing, Morgan threw himself into bed, narrowly missing the wooden post near his pillow. One more day of avoiding eye contact. Another training session filled with no more than grunts and an occasional order, followed by a lonely supper in his study. The night would be no different than those in the weeks prior, full of restless sleep and nightmares that now included the look of panic on that beautiful face after what had been the most wonderful moment of Morgan's entire existence. He choked back a sob, burying his face in his sheets.

Is this to be your life henceforth? Absent of the one person who gives you hope? Who gives you purpose?

Arthur had kissed *him*. Morgan had kept his restraint. He had shoved everything to the darkest depths of his mind, content to be his prince's stalwart companion and ally until the end of days, lifting the man up to fulfill his destiny no matter how it pained him. Yet, there he lay, filled with unease at the notion that they might never share even comfortable conversation again.

You cannot go on like this, le Fay. You must find a way to let go.

A gentle knock—two times, a familiar request made only by one person—came at the door to his bedchamber. Morgan's pulse quickened, eyes snapping open in an instant. "Come... come in."

Light spilled into the room, defining the broad shoulders and hesitant stance of his prince's figure. "Did I wake you?"

"No," Morgan croaked, shifting upright to sit against the frame of his bed. "Sleep eludes me."

Arthur shut the door behind him, pausing briefly where he stood. "Can... can we speak? Please?"

Morgan's breath faltered at the ache in the Prince's voice. He longed to interact with the man as they used to, yearning for even a semblance of what they had been so many months ago. "Of course, Your Highness."

Arthur's shoulders sagged at the honorific, but he turned, latching the door behind him. Morgan's brows jumped at the urgency in the movements. He pointed a finger at the candle at his bedside, lighting it with a faint glint of violet.

"Do not think me unable to hear the detachment in your voice when you address me as such, Morgan," he snapped, moving to stand at the foot of his bed, leaning against the post with his arms crossed. "I've come to loathe the title on your lips."

Morgan bit his lip, taken aback by the frustration in his voice. It was true, he had resorted to referring to him as "Your Highness" of late in an attempt to push him away, simply to let himself heal. He'd never meant to hurt Arthur with it.

The prince scowled down at him, saying nothing and chewing the inside of his cheek. Morgan's brows raised higher. "Sparkling conversation, this."

"Oh, shut it," Arthur grumbled, running a hand through his hair. Pain crossed his features for a moment. He opened his mouth and closed it again, fumbling for words. Finally, he gestured to the bed. "May I?"

Morgan shrugged, pulling his knees to his chest to make room. "As Your Highness wishes."

"Please stop." His eyes pressed shut, the hurt there more pronounced. "Morgan... I don't... I can't do this anymore. Pretending everything is right between us, acting as if you are simply my father's ward and nothing more to me. Every day that I am forced to share nothing but orders and terse nods of understanding with you..." He opened his eyes, staring at Morgan with such deep sorrow that it wrapped around his heart and squeezed. "It breaks my heart. I miss you."

"What would you ask of me?" Morgan's breath hitched in his chest, and he turned his head, quickly wiping away a stray tear. "My acting skills pale in comparison to the fools. I can only feign inner peace so well, Arthur."

"I..." Arthur's voice broke, reaching out as Morgan pulled his hand away. He heaved a sigh. "Morgan... I swear, I never meant to cause you heartache. I know my actions these past months have been trying. I opened a door that day that I cannot close, but I..." Tears welled in his eyes as he leaned closer. "Morgan, please look at me."

He drew a rattling breath, slowly turning to face the Prince. "I don't want to close that door, Morgan."

Morgan searched his face. His lips opened as he stared at Arthur, questioning his hearing, sure that he had misunderstood. "Wh-What?"

A grin tugged one corner of the Prince's lips. "I do not regret kissing you, Morgan le Fay."

Morgan's heart swelled, certain he was dreaming. Certain he had found sleep or that the fae had managed their way into his head again, toying with his thoughts. "What... does that mean?"

Arthur shrugged, looking toward the fire where it still crackled in the hearth. "It means that I've been lying to myself these moons past. That I've caused you unnecessary pain while I selfishly withdrew to reconcile my thoughts." He turned back to Morgan, pleading in his eyes. "Can you forgive me?"

Another tear trailed down Morgan's cheek. He nodded, smiling. "Always, my prince."

Arthur smiled wide, shifting closer to him on the bed. "I much prefer that title on your lips." He reached out again, asking this time.

Morgan chuckled, taking his hand.

"I don't... truly know what that means for us, Morgan," Arthur whispered, bringing his hand to his lips to brush his knuckles. "I wish I had an answer for you."

Sadness flooded him, knowing fully the weight of Arthur's responsibilities. He nodded weakly. "I... understand, Arthur."

"You don't." The Prince shook his head, smiling. "I have done a lot of thinking while we were... strained. And I will admit that I am... drawn to you..." Arthur swallowed hard. "As far more than simply your friend."

Morgan choked a sob, hardly daring to believe the moment was real, fighting to seal the gaps in his defenses even as Arthur leaned into him. Their breaths began to mingle as his prince whispered against his lips, "I want all of you, Morgan le Fay, and if I am too late..." His crystal blue eyes danced in the candlelight, overflowing with desire. "Then I will take whatever parts of yourself you are willing to give."

The cracks in his armor gave way, and Morgan's lips crashed into Arthur's. Light and warmth wrapped around his beating heart as they pressed deeper into one another. His lips parted, allowing the Prince's tongue to pass. He took Arthur's jaw in his hand, sinking into him with a hum. His lips were silk and honey, sweet and addictive. His skin was fire, heat against his palm to comfort the coldest reaches of his heart. He wanted more.

Morgan shifted forward, placing his knees on either side of Arthur's lap to straddle his waist. His prince had not been lying, his want laid bare by the hardened length that now pressed against Morgan's beneath their clothing.

Morgan gasped, suddenly filled with the weight of the moment as he pulled back, staring into Arthur's eyes.

"Shhh..." Arthur whispered, running a hand through Morgan's hair. "No more pretending, Morgan. I want this. I want *you.*"

He had longed to hear those words for what felt like a lifetime now, yet it did nothing but stoke the fear in his chest.

"Do you want me?" Arthur breathed, "Do you want your prince, Morgan? I will be yours so long as you let me."

"Yes," Morgan gasped. "For so very long, Arthur."

Arthur met his lips again, slowly, over and over. "Do you trust me?"

Morgan swallowed, clinging to Arthur's neck. "With my life."

Arthur smiled, cradling the back of Morgan's neck to rest his head against the pillows. "And your body?" he whispered, running his fingers beneath Morgan's shirt, trailing over the cut valleys of his stomach to stoke the fire in his groin.

"Yes," Morgan rasped, trembling with fear and want. "With all of me."

Arthur tugged at the hem, coaxing the shirt up and over Morgan's torso. He dipped down, peppering his moonlit skin with kisses across the fine hairs surrounding his navel. Morgan shuddered, finding one of the Prince's hands to intertwine their fingers as Arthur explored his body with his lips.

"Arthur..." he whimpered, shaking as the man trailed up his chest, teasing at one of his nipples and flitting his tongue over it.

"So sweet," the Prince whispered, his heated breath washing over his skin. He moved up, caressing Morgan's throat with his lips and teeth. "I've been so unfair to you, my sweet boy. Let me make amends. Let me take care of you."

Morgan's head lolled back as Arthur's tongue trailed over his neck, lightning surging through every part of him. "P-Please. Kiss me, Arthur."

His prince did as he asked, nipping at his lower lip with every pull. "You're so beautiful, Morgan. I can't believe it took me so long to see it."

A laugh bubbled out of him, and Arthur pulled back, smirking. "What? I speak the truth."

Morgan smiled, tugging at his jaw to kiss him again. "I've always thought you were a sight to behold. Since we were but scrawny youths on the training field."

"I know," Arthur whispered, clearing his throat at the scowl Morgan gave him. "I caught you staring in the barracks. It was one of the things I've been thinking on lately."

"How so?" Morgan asked, flushing.

"Well, I suppose I never said anything because... it never upset me. I felt rather flattered. Excited, even. I've only recently been capable of admitting it, however. I'm sorry, Morgan."

"Stop apologizing, Arthur," Morgan groaned, pressing another kiss to his lips. "These aren't ideal circumstances. And we've all made our peace with the notion that our beloved prince can be a bit... simple sometimes."

Arthur dipped down, growling through his grin. "Bite your tongue, peasant."

Morgan giggled, grabbing his neck. "Bite it for me, Your Highness."

"Cheeky imp," Arthur scoffed, devouring his mouth with a rumble in his chest. His hands ran over Morgan's chest and down his stomach, lingering at his waist. "May I? Please?" he begged into the kiss.

Morgan smiled, taking Arthur's shirt in his fingers to pry it from his skin. "Now you may."

Arthur chuckled, moving down to his neck again as he worked the laces on Morgan's trousers. "I want to see all of you," he whispered. "Taste all of you."

Morgan trembled at his words, every one of his deepest and darkest desires coming to life. "I'm yours," he gasped, "All of me."

Arthur ran his palm over Morgan's aching cock where it pressed against the bindings. Morgan groaned, rolling upwards into the touch. A sharp breath escaped his throat as Arthur slipped his fingers beneath the fabric, taking him in his hand to stroke him gently. "So hard," Arthur growled into his ear, "So eager for your prince."

Morgan had lost himself completely, undone by the man's touch. "Arthur... fuck, Ar—"

Arthur caught his lips again, swallowing his curses up greedily. "Shh... not so loud."

Wholly uncertain he could comply, Morgan's eyes snapped open, irises glowing violet as a ripple wafted through the air. Arthur stayed his hand, still gripping Morgan's length as his brows raised in question.

Morgan panted, smirking, "Now we needn't worry about being overheard."

A wicked grin crossed Arthur's lips. He sidled down the bed, bringing Morgan's hips to his face. Both of his hands slid over Morgan's ass, earning a whimper as he pulled his trousers down, allowing his swollen cock to slap against his stomach.

Arthur stared, eyes flitting between Morgan's face and his shaft. He bit his lip, dipping down to press his tongue to the head, lapping up the beads he'd already drawn from him.

Morgan's head fell back, gasping for air as the Prince ran his lips and tongue from the base to the tip.

"So beautiful..." Arthur whispered against his skin, staring up at him as he swallowed him whole.

Morgan threaded his fingers into Arthur's hair, bucking deeper into his mouth to the back of his throat. "Fuck... Fuck yes, Arthur. My gods, that feels so good. So right."

"It is right, Morgan..." Arthur panted, kissing his cock before moving to his thigh in a desperate need to have his lips on every portion of his skin, "I've never been more certain."

Still stroking him, faster now with the slickness left from his mouth, Arthur traced a finger along the flesh beneath his sack. Morgan tensed, looking down at him with ravenous want.

"Not tonight..." Arthur whispered, moving up to catch his lips again, running his knuckles along his jaw. "I will have you, my sweet boy," he said at the sudden hurt in Morgan's eyes, "but tonight is about you. And rest assured that when I fuck you, it will be a day to remember."

Morgan's mind blanked at the promise, nearly coming in his prince's hand from the thought alone. "As if this night could ever be forgotten."

"Most certainly not," the Prince uttered, trailing his lips back down Morgan's body to finish what he started, "but I did say that I wanted every part of you."

"Oh, fuck! Arthur!" Morgan gasped as the Prince's tongue flitted between his ass cheeks, teasing.

Arthur rumbled a laugh, adding enough sensation to drive him wild. With a few more strokes of his tongue, he pressed a finger against his hole, gently circling the ring of muscle.

Morgan was melting, pulling at his own hair as his body shook. Arthur's finger slipped into him. His back arched at the intrusion, fighting with himself to relax. Arthur's lips locked around his aching cock again, dividing Morgan's focus to allow the prince deeper inside.

With his free hand, Arthur undid the bindings on his own trousers, and Morgan fought through the pleasure wracking him to glimpse his prince's cock come free. A whimper escaped him at the sight, wanting nothing more than to taste it, to feel Arthur inside him.

"Please..." Morgan panted. "I want you, Arthur."

Arthur grinned, stroking himself as he slipped a second finger into his hole. "You are desperately testing my resolve, little imp."

"Please," Morgan moaned, biting his lip as he stared down.

"No," Arthur said firmly. "I have never wanted like I want you, Morgan le Fay. I will prove myself to you, give you everything you deserve. If I am to claim you, then I shall do it properly."

Morgan managed a smirk, his heart filling with warmth at the notion to drive away his disappointment. "I would hardly call this proper," he moaned. "Your fingers are buried in my ass."

Arthur pressed deeper, causing his vision to flare white and his nerves to sing. "And I suggest you remember it."

The Prince leaned down, taking Morgan's cock in his mouth once more as he stroked himself with one hand and stretched Morgan with the other. Morgan cried out, latching onto Arthur's head as heat pooled in his stomach. The Prince pumped himself faster, sensing Morgan's urgency at the roll of his hips.

Arthur let out a groan, catching up to Morgan as they chased their releases together.

"Arthur! Fuck, Arthur, I'm—" Morgan heaved, stars bursting behind his eyes. The Prince hollowed his cheeks, sucking him down as he flooded his mouth.

Arthur roared into the fine hairs at Morgan's waist, spilling onto the bed between their legs. Panting as he pulled off of Morgan's cock with a pop, he stilled, licking his lips. His head rested against Morgan's thigh before staring up at him, eyes sparkling. "My sweet boy."

Morgan chuckled, reaching out for him. Arthur climbed up and into his arms, sagging into his chest. Heat built between their spent bodies where their skin connected, filling Morgan with peace. He tugged at Arthur's chin with his fingers, ushering him up to his lips to taste himself on the man's tongue.

"Stay with me?" he asked with a whisper.

Arthur nodded, tucking his head against Morgan's neck. "We've spent many a night in each other's chambers. I suspect the castle will simply be glad to know we're speaking again."

Morgan pressed a kiss into his hair, smiling so wide it hurt his face. "Are you alright?"

Arthur pulled back, grinning. "I have never been better, Morgan. I made my peace with my desires weeks ago. I simply had to find the nerve to come to you." He met Morgan's lips, humming with delight at their touch. "Whatever comes of this... we face it together."

Morgan swallowed, choking back the words that tried to climb up his throat—words he had been certain of long before his prince dared to kiss him. He nodded, pressing his forehead to Arthur's. "Together."

Our first full short takes place several weeks after the scene prior. Arthur has a promise to keep, and our Crown Prince means to sweep his witch off his feet.

Literally.

This short was released on July 31st, 2024

Said the Stars

Camelot - The Reign of His Majesty, Uther Pendragon

"Guinevere, what in the deepest circle is this about?" Morgan groaned, glaring at the Princess over a market stall as she picked through elaborate silks and fine linens, occasionally holding one up to the light.

The townspeople had flocked to the market that morning as seasonal traders from across the land convened for harvest. He understood the allure. It was far more convenient, selecting his own purchases, than sending servants out with a list. Not that any of the servants were permitted to do more for him than clean or summon him to the few audiences he was expected to attend.

None of the castle staff truly harbored any ill toward Morgan. Many had tried to show kindness over the years, but the threat of being dismissed by Uther, should he learn of their disobedience, simply wasn't worth the risk. At that time, there was no need for them to interact with him at all. He cleaned his own chambers, fetched his own meals from the kitchen, and even made a point to write down the dates of important gatherings should his presence be required. No one would suffer on his behalf if he could prevent it.

Guinevere, however, was doted upon by all. While she didn't care for the attention, stubbornly independent as she was, she had been raised a royal. And as a long-term guest from Knucklas since her betrothal to Arthur, she knew better than to spurn any kindness shown.

Therefore, Morgan became instantly suspicious when she had whisked him away from his morning studies to peruse the stalls for the makings of a new dress. Despite the staff's eagerness to provide for her at every turn, he knew all too well that she'd rather don a suit of armor than own yet another frock. "You have three dresses in that shade already, and upon seeing the most recent, I believe your exact words were 'Oh lovely, I'll match the pumpkins perfectly for the harvest festival.'"

Gwen shot him a smirk, setting the fabric down. "Why so irritable today, darling? You love the market."

"I enjoy new books, trinkets and occasionally a tunic that won't drown me," he huffed, glancing around as people entered and left his space over and again. "The numerous crossings of personal boundaries, I can do without."

Guinevere giggled, covering her lips with her fingertips. "Come along, you silly curmudgeon. I believe I saw a cart with an assortment of comfits. Something sweet always quells your ire."

"Guinevere..." he growled, pushing through the crowd to follow. The notion of crystallized strew berries may have added a slight skip to his step, but as they walked down the main path in the center of the field where the market was held, the castle rose into view.

Morgan's eyes instinctively went to the arched window of the highest floor's eastern wing. Even from the distance, he could sometimes make out the shadow that would pace the chamber. Though, it had ceased lurking there as often as it once had in the months prior.

"My sweet boy..."

His fingers unconsciously found his lips, recalling the warmth, the heat, the delicious, sticky taste of his prince's kiss. A whisper of euphoria embraced his chest, those stars bursting behind his eyes at Arthur's command, his body completely at his whim.

It happened again on the night that followed. And the night after that, stealing as many moments in the dark as they were able. Exploring each other, learning one another's body as if it were their own. Morgan had always desired to bask in Arthur's presence, but this—this was incessant. In mere weeks, his prince had become an addiction.

A vice now unquestionably shared.

Yet, Arthur had made a promise. A vow, spoken in whispered breaths against Morgan's cock as he took him apart with his fingers.

Romance. Courtship, even. The intent, however, was beyond his understanding. It wasn't as if he and his prince could ever truly be together in this life. Such a dream required a fortress to hold it—to imprison it, for this world would never survive should it break free.

"I assure you," Gwen chimed, lacing an arm through his elbow and leaning in, "he isn't sulking in his chambers today, Morgan."

He tore his eyes away. "I... who? What do you mean?"

"Oh, don't play games." She swatted his arm. "Never have I seen the light that lives on your faces these past weeks. Stop tormenting me, would you? Tell me what's happened with Arthur."

"A *princess* ought be a modicum less brazen when she suggests an affair between her betrothed and another man, don't you think?" Morgan grinned, gliding away toward the cart of sweets.

"An *affair?!*" Gwen squealed with delight, drawing far too much attention.

Morgan shot her a wide-eyed stare with tight lips.

She glanced around at the townsfolk, rolling her eyes as she hurried after him. "Are you telling me that you two have... that you've been—"

"*Guinevere*," he scathed, handing the gentleman at the cart a few coins in exchange for a small woven pouch bursting with candied berries.

"Calm yourself, would you?" She huffed. "No one would believe such a tale to begin with. You could drag Arthur from the castle, throw your arms around him right here and ki—"

Morgan promptly shoved one of the berries between her lips to silence her.

She laughed, holding a hand over her mouth. "I must truly be driving you mad if you're sharing your sweets."

"Why are we here, Guinevere?" Morgan growled. "You don't want a new dress. You *never* want a new dress."

Gwen swallowed, licking her lips with a smile. "You share. Then I'll share. That's our arrangement, isn't it?"

Morgan heaved a sigh, throwing his head back. He and the Princess had a bit of a pact. Their romantic lives, both sordid and easily weaponized should the wrong person learn of them, were spoken of in turn so that they each had someone to confide in.

He jerked his head toward the path that led back to the castle. His eyes shimmered violet as they walked, muffling their voices. "He came to my room several weeks ago. Said he couldn't stand the way things had become between us since that moment in the storeroom, that he... missed me."

"Took him long enough." She rolled her eyes, holding out a hand for another berry.

Morgan obliged, all too relieved to be getting things off his chest. "He... uh..."

"Before Arthur and I are forced to marry, *please*, Morgan."

A laugh escaped his nose. "He kissed me again. And... then things got rather... intense."

Guinevere was practically skipping. "Intense? Did you fuck?"

"Dear *gods*, what sort of princess are you, exactly?"

"The sort this world is in desperate need of," she snapped. "Answer the question."

"No," Morgan groaned. "Not... not quite, but..." he let out an airy breath, clutching his purchase to his chest. "It was the best night of my entire existence, Guinevere. I've never felt so... *complete* before. As if all pretenses had finally been swept away and we could be ourselves."

The princess's face was glowing with the smile she wore, saying nothing as they drew closer to the castle.

"We've... been meeting as often as we can since," he continued. "Some nights simply holding one another. Others are... well... *filthy*."

Guinevere belted a laugh. "But you haven't..."

Morgan shook his head, biting his lip. "Arthur said he wants to do it *properly*, whatever that means. I certainly doubt he intends to *marry*, so I've not a notion what's in his head."

"He has done some outrageous things for you in the past," she chuckled, "and the way he smiles at you lately, Morgan..." She shook her head. "He's never looked at anyone—"

"Don't," he interrupted gently. "Please don't, Gwen. I cannot... let myself think that way. Whatever Arthur is able to give... I will take. But... if I hope..."

"I know," she whispered, taking his hand with a sad smile. "I know, my sweet, sweet Morgan. However, if you will not let yourself hope—then I shall hope for you."

Morgan laughed softly.

"Now then..." Guinevere said, "I was asked to distract you for a time."

"Wh-What?" he stammered. "Whatever for? By whom?"

"He gave me no details, simply asked that I keep you out of the castle for a short time. The King left early for the conclave this morning. Arthur has given the staff the day off in his absence, and..." Gwen's smile overtook her entire face. "...he's waiting for you."

Cinder and pine blanketed the crisp air with comforting warmth from the hearth. The castle's finest linens draped a delicately carved oak table, laden with dishes to make even royalty break all standards of their upbringing with drool on their lips. It wasn't a standard midday meal, however.

Fat sausages. Baked apples. One of the finest cheeses that had been tucked away in the larder for a special occasion. A cask of blackberry wine, fermented with ginger. And a heaping mound of egg-soaked bread, crisped in butter and a hint of cinnamon, smothered in honey.

While not a dish served in Camelot, Arthur had mentioned hearing of it during a short stay in one of the southern kingdoms, and he'd retained a mental image of the way Morgan had licked his lips at the idea.

His father would most certainly have been irate at the sight of his son, the future king, partaking in sweets for lunch. That was, if he hadn't already fainted at the notion of Morgan, a witch, a man, being the central focus of his efforts to prepare such a meal. Although, the crown prince slaving in the castle kitchen might have been enough to send him reeling.

Arthur was no stranger to cooking. Roasting meat over a fire, even preparing a basic stew was a necessary survival skill for any soldier. But the Prince thoroughly enjoyed his culinary comforts when he was able, and the only person he'd ever been able to share his deep fondness for food with was his Morgan.

And Morgan was indeed his. How that was to play out in the future may have still been in the early stages of planning. Royals had always maintained their secrets over the ages—their quirks and their eccentricities. If anyone were to understand and allow such an entanglement beyond their matrimony, it would be Guinevere. After all, he held suspicions that she herself may have been in love with another, even should she maintain propriety in his presence.

But his witch deserved more. More than hushed moments in the dark and stolen throes of passion. Morgan deserved courtship. He deserved poetry and song, heart-spoken proclamation and praise to spurn the gods themselves.

Morgan deserved a true place at his side.

Arthur shook the fanciful daydreams from his mind, fiddling with an ivory toggle that adorned a silk tunic. He had scoffed at the garment when it had been brought to him nearly a year ago, his father's notions of masculinity echoing an opinion unlike his own.

Morgan, however, had noticed it one day while rousing him from a late sleep, rifling through his closet to get him dressed in time for training.

"I believe you might stun the people into silence wearing this," he had said, laughing.

"Ostentatious, isn't it?" Arthur had replied.

"No, Arthur... it's beautiful," he'd sang, fully claiming the Prince's attention. "Paired with everything that you are, I doubt a soul could tear their eyes away."

Arthur had thought nothing of it, wholly unbothered by his dearest friend's clear flirtation. In fact, the sentiment had made him feel rather glorious for the rest of the morning.

"A simple prince, indeed, Arthur Pendragon," he muttered to himself, tousling his hair.

A knock came at the door, and his heart leapt into his throat. He glanced around the room in haste, double checking his preparations. With a nod, he reached for a single rose that lay on the table, and made to open the door with a smile.

Morgan's eyes swelled. His jaw dropped, looking Arthur up and down. "Arthur... you look absolutely stunning."

An elated laugh left the prince's throat as he moved close, taking Morgan's hands to pull him into the room. "Said the stars unto the moon."

His witch sputtered a gasp. He tripped over his own feet, falling forward into Arthur's chest, crushing the rose between them. "Oh—hells, I'm so sorry. My gods, Arthur, what you said—that was *beautiful*. Wherever did you hear it?"

"In my head," he chuckled, brushing a lock of hair from Morgan's brow. "You said something the other night while we were in your bed... *radiant*, I think you called me."

Morgan stifled a laugh. "You had spend on your cheek, your hair was absurd, and we were both drenched in sweat." He shrugged. "There was no other word for it."

"Mhm," Arthur hummed, gently nudging his lips with his own. "And I thought, 'How dare he? How maddeningly disrespectful—*treasonous* even, that he lay there, looking like the stars themselves made flesh with honeyed words on his tongue for *me*.'"

"Arthur, honestly, this food smells heavenly." Morgan pressed a finger to his lips. "Please don't force me to let it go cold whilst I ravish you on the floor."

Arthur kissed his fingers, chuckling. "Oh, you wouldn't dare, Morgan le Fay. Take a look."

Morgan tore his eyes away, gazing at the table. He inhaled sharply, light blossoming on his face. "Is that... did you..."

"I did, indeed," Arthur whispered, wrapping his arms around his witch from behind.

Morgan spun around in his embrace, staring at him in amazement. "All of this..." He looked down at the battered rose, still between Arthur's fingers. Violet sparkled in his eyes, and the flower regained its proper shape, blooming fully as life surged through its petals. "...for me?"

His prince held the rose between their bodies, taking a deep whiff of the fragrance. "Would that I could give you the world, my sweet boy... my shining star. But I have only food, flowers and fanciful words. Forgive your simple prince?"

Taking the rose in one hand and fisting the other into the silk tunic, Morgan pulled him into a bruising kiss. Fierce and desperate at first—a fire roaring to life, only to wain into slow, delicate flames, tender and warm.

Pulling away with a gentle hum, he breathed, "All I desire... all I have ever wanted is you."

Arthur's face lit with a glowing smile. "Granted."

Their meal sparkled with laughter, flirtation and easy conversation. Such was always the way with his very best of friends. Arthur recounted the way the kitchen staff had gawked at him in disbelief when he began preparing the food while they gathered their belongings to leave for the day. Morgan nearly spat out his wine as the Prince put a sausage to his lips, sliding his tongue along the length before popping the entire morsel into his mouth.

When their bellies were full, Arthur began clearing the table. Morgan stood to help, only for his hand to be swatted away.

"I am taking care of *you* today." Arthur grinned, stacking their empty dishes. "Go collect your cloak and wait for me at the entry hall."

"So..." Morgan leaned over Arthur's shoulder as their horse carried them into the Brecillian Wood, headed toward their special place along the river. "Is this what you meant when you said you intended to do this properly?"

The Prince's body shook with silent laughter in his embrace. "Oh, I haven't impressed you yet, then?"

He felt his face flush, a sensation that rarely occurred. "N-No! That's not what I—"

"I merely jest, Morgan," Arthur chuckled. "It is still *me*, you know. Your *friend*. The prince you've made a habit of taunting your entire life. Because we've grown intimate doesn't mean all of that is forgotten."

"I know that, you simpleton," Morgan growled. The babble of the river met his ears, and they dipped down a slope marked with colorful fabrics hung on low branches.

Arthur shook his head as they reached the water's edge. He leapt from the horse, offering his hand. "Good. I wouldn't know how to go on without that sour pout on your lips to make me smile every now and again."

Morgan rolled his eyes, allowing the prince to help him down. Arthur grinned, tying the reins to a large oak—their oak, carved with the letters A and M.

Running his fingertips over the markings, Morgan smiled to himself. "It surprises me sometimes, you know? I expected it to be more difficult."

"What is that?" the Prince cast him a glance with raised brows.

"This. You and I." Morgan dropped his hand from the bark, turning to face him. "When we kiss, it's as if it was always meant to be that way—my lips on yours. When we fight side by side on the battlefield, there is nothing that can stand against us. I suppose... I try too hard to separate who we're meant to be in the eyes of the kingdom and who we truly are. The ease at which our two worlds seem to slip into one another frightens me."

Arthur's face sank. He patted the horse, reaching into the pack he'd prepared to extract several blankets. Without a word, he strode across the clearing, layering the fabrics over the long, flat boulder in the center. He sat, placing his palm on the padding beside him. "Come here, my sweet boy."

The look in his prince's eyes pulled him to his side, longing, sorrow and restraint all tangled up together. Arthur wrapped a hand around his waist, holding him tight. "I wish for our forever, you know."

Morgan's eyes snapped to his. "You do?"

Arthur nodded, staring out across the river. "A day when those two worlds can become one, and no one would harbor anything but happiness for us. An endless night when the stars and their moon can whisper to one another without fear of the sun rising to steal the sky away."

"Say the word, my prince," Morgan said, resting his head on Arthur's shoulder. "Say the word and I will find a way to snuff out the sun."

Arthur chuckled, tilting down to kiss his lips. "I don't doubt that you could, Morgan. Not for a second."

"I want that as well, Arthur," he whispered, brushing his knuckles along the Prince's jaw. "But know that so long as the sun continues to rise, forcing the stars and the moon to hide..." Morgan pulled Arthur close by the back of his neck, crushing their lips together. "They yet remain, even if out of sight."

The Prince's eyes danced in the dim light of the clearing, searching Morgan's. "Morgan, I... I..."

A silent gasp swept through Morgan's thinly parted lips. His heart hammered in his chest, thrumming at the words fighting to free themselves from Arthur's tongue.

Arthur sighed, then smiled. "Yes."

"Wh... What?"

"This is indeed what I meant by doing things properly."

Morgan's brows shot up. "You... you mean..." His heart now fought to break free of his ribcage for an entirely different, yet not altogether unwelcome reason. "Here? In the clearing?"

"Yes, my sweet boy," Arthur growled, ushering him to lay back on the bedding. He crawled over him, staring down with fire in his eyes. "I want all of you. Right here, in our own small world."

Morgan swallowed nervously even as his blood raced between his legs. He wanted to give himself to Arthur more than anything. To actually feel his prince inside him.

"You have all of me, Arthur..." Morgan breathed, Arthur's lips brushing over his, teasing. "You always have."

"I would give anything to say those words to you, Morgan." Arthur's hands quickly undid the fastenings on Morgan's tunic and breeches. His hands slid beneath the cotton, trailing up the valleys of his stomach, sending prickles of lightning over his skin. "But I swear to you, that whatever I have to offer, every shred of my heart that I can steal away from crown and kingdom..." Arthur ran his tongue up his throat, from his collarbone to his ear, making him groan. "...is *yours*."

"That is all..." Morgan breathed, gasping between his words as Arthur's lips, tongue and teeth drove him wild, "...I have ever wanted, my prince. More than I could have ever dreamed."

Arthur tugged Morgan's boots free, followed quickly by his breeches. His tunic went next, leaving him bare, laid out atop the boulder for his prince.

Sitting back to stare, Arthur wet his lips. "So beautiful..." His hands slid down Morgan's chest, over his hips to grip his thighs. "Lie back for me, sweetheart. Let me have this gorgeous ass." The Prince squeezed both cheeks firmly, kneeling on the ground.

Morgan laid back on the soft blankets, gazing up through the treetops as Arthur lifted his legs with a push behind his knees. His breath caught in his chest as a wet finger slipped between his cheeks.

"Keep an ear out for any movement while I make you squirm for me, beautiful." The prince growled, kissing and nipping at his inner thighs. He leant down, dragging his tongue from the base of Morgan's rigid cock all the way to the tip.

"I... don't know what you expect me to do," Morgan panted, eyes rolling back in his head as a finger teased his ass. "Repeat what you did with your tongue the other night, and any creature within a mile will hear me scream."

Arthur met his eyes with a wicked grin. "Very well, then. No tongue."

"Stow the chaff and put that mouth to better use, Your Highness," Morgan rasped, eyes blazing with violet light.

A soft pulse shimmered through the clearing, muting any sound within. He craned his neck to the side, casting another spell at the base of the slope that led to the space. Any who came within a hundred feet of them would find themselves fleeing in the other direction, overcome with inexplicable terror.

"That's my boy," Arthur snickered before dragging his tongue from Morgan's tailbone all the way to his balls.

"Oh, fuck..." Morgan shuddered, twisting his fingers into the blankets.

Arthur lapped and sucked, kissed and bit his way along every inch of skin, pulling filthy sounds from Morgan he wasn't even aware himself capable of making until recently.

Every single one seemed to spur the Prince on, lancing him with his tongue, rumbling ravenous growls in his throat.

"Arthur..." Morgan moaned, eyes rolling back in his skull. "Oil... did you—"

"The pack," Arthur said quickly, never deviating from his task. One hand still firm on his ass, he undid the laces on his own trousers, reaching inside to pull his cock free.

Morgan craned back toward where the horse was tied, eyeing the pack with violet in his irises. A dark bottle flew through the air, landing softly in the grass beside Arthur's knee.

Pressing soft kisses along Morgan's leg, Arthur breathed, "Open yourself up for me, sweetheart. Let me watch." He pulled back long enough to remove his tunic and drop his breeches. Collecting the oil from the ground, he dropped a generous amount of the liquid into his palm, running it over his length before coating Morgan's ass with the rest.

Morgan bit his lip, fixed on his prince's hungry stare as he reached between his legs. With a single finger, he pushed inside himself.

Arthur groaned as he moved forward, arching Morgan's ass upward with his legs over his shoulders. "Another, sweet boy. You can do it."

Nodding, Morgan added a second digit, trembling as he stretched further, aching for his prince to replace his fingers. "Arthur... my Arthur..."

"Absolutely beautiful..." Arthur whispered, kissing every inch of skin his lips could find. He knelt down, running his tongue over Morgan's stomach where his cock had already begun to leak, moaning with delight as he licked his lips. His own finger danced alongside Morgan's, and he raised a brow.

"Yes..." Morgan whimpered, desperate for Arthur to be inside him in any way.

"Relax, sweetheart," the Prince uttered, carefully pushing in, working together to open him wide. "That's it."

"Ugh... oh gods, fuck..." Morgan bit his lip hard, holding back every blasphemous word that tried to rip free. "Arthur... please..."

Arthur chuckled softly, guiding both of their hands away. He moved between Morgan's legs, leaning in to cradle the back of his neck. "You are mine, Morgan le Fay. Now and forever, do you understand me?"

Tears prickled their way into Morgan's lashes, his heart ready to burst. Those words were the closest thing he would ever hear to the ones he longed to say himself, and he would hold tight to them. "Now and forever."

Arthur pressed the head of his cock against Morgan's ass. His fingers curled in his hair, their lips locked in an all-consuming kiss, and Arthur pushed.

Morgan cried out, a sound immediately devoured by his prince as he slid inside. Pleasure and pain clashed within, only for a moment before they combined to create glorious sensations he'd never imagined.

"My Morgan..." Arthur whispered between kisses, holding him to his chest as their bodies slowly moved along one another. "My sweet, beautiful boy, you are *bliss*."

Arthur reached deeper and deeper with every thrust. Morgan latched his arms around the Prince's neck, grounding himself before he could float away. The smell of musty earth and fresh water mingled together with the scent of the man above, taking him whole. Lighting raced through his veins. Fire tore over his flesh where their bodies connected, and stars exploded behind his eyes.

"Arthur..." Morgan choked, kissing him over and over again, knotting his fingers in that golden hair and wishing he could pull him impossibly closer. "I... Arthur... I..."

Don't. Please don't say it. Do not set it free.

"Morgan..." Arthur's eyes swelled above him, wide and begging.

"*I need you...*" Morgan pleaded, yearning for all of his prince, yet refusing to let himself say the words. "I need you, Arthur..."

"I'm here, Morgan," Arthur breathed, clutching him tighter to his chest, fucking him faster and harder, doing everything in his power to give him what he asked without knowing the depth of his need. "I'm yours."

His vision turned white as Arthur shifted, ramming his cock so deep inside that Morgan's entire body lit like the sun itself. Heat coiled in his belly. Whimpering cries of utmost pleasure jutted from his throat with every slap of skin. "Arthur... I'm right there. So close."

Arthur's jaw fell, panting in time with his witch. "Come for me, sweetheart. I want to see you come just from taking my cock."

The command sent lust coursing through every fiber of Morgan's being, pushing him over the edge. Hot, wet bursts shot up his stomach—another over his chest and up his neck. Arthur dipped down, sucking every drop he could reach from his skin without leaving his ass. "Yes... Yes, my sweet boy."

"Arthur..." Morgan melted in his embrace, tingling from head to toe and trembling as Arthur rammed into him with purpose. His lashes fluttered in a daze while he sought his prince's lips. "Come inside me. Please, Arthur. Like... like I'm yours."

"You are..." Arthur heaved, his voice cracking as beads of sweat rolled down his jaw. "You are mine, *fy cariad.*" The Prince's abdominal muscles tensed. The roll of his hips became sharp, and he roared through gritted teeth, grunting into the crook of Morgan's neck.

A stuttered moan left Morgan's throat as warmth coated him from the inside. He wrapped his hands around Arthur's back, holding him tight as his body convulsed. Again. And again, until he became still in his arms.

Morgan's mind raced in spite of his exhaustion.

Fy cariad. He... he called you—his heart.

"Morgan?" Arthur's eyes were fixed on his face, staring up from his chest.

"Hmm?" he hummed, coming back to himself.

"I meant it," the Prince said forcefully.

Morgan's heart leapt into his throat. "Wh-What?"

"That you are mine and I am yours," Arthur said, kissing his chest. "As much and as often as I am able."

Yours—with conditions. He was merely caught up in the moment. Don't wallow, le Fay. Live in this with him. Your heart is going to break. Let it break it spectacularly.

His doubt rested not in Arthur's intentions, nor his affections for him. He simply knew that a prince, destined as Arthur Pendragon was, and a witch stood little chance of combating their fate and changing the world they lived in.

Nodding and smiling, he trailed his fingertips over Arthur's jaw. "I believe you, my prince."

With another kiss, Arthur pulled out of him, standing to retrieve their clothes. Morgan scanned the blankets, searching for something to clean the mess off his stomach. When he made to get to his feet, Arthur said, "Don't. Stay right there."

Morgan snapped his head up at the urgency in his voice, finding the prince frozen in his tracks and staring. Sunbeams filtered down through the branches over his olive skin, highlighting every cut of his body, glistening with sweat. Glowing.

"What is it?" Morgan muttered.

"You." Arthur smiled, shaking his head. "Radiant you."

Belting a laugh, Morgan dropped back onto the blankets, more than happy to let his prince stare. "Said the stars unto the moon."

For those unfamiliar with the finer details of Arthurian Lore, Etna was the mountain to which the enchantress Morgan le Fay stole away with the body of Arthur Pendragon after he fell on the fields of Camlaan. While the events of our Morgan's life may have differed greatly, he accepts that he is to live his life beneath that mountain's shadow.

Days after waking from his tomb, a ghostly companion in his head, even the name he chooses reflects that knowledge...

...for "Fell" means "One who lives in the shadow of the mountain."

This short was released on January 23rd, 2024

Shadow of the Mountain

07.23.198 UI

"Etna..." A dark figure swathed in simple garments stalked along dark, stone rivers between towering, modern-day castles. Hair black as the surrounding night clung to his neck, slick with sweat and coated in sand brought from the wastes—a vast sea of barren nothingness that comprised almost the entirety of the world beyond the city walls. "An iron hellscape in place of the mountain's majesty? What a sad world."

The dank, cold air of that ancient tomb was almost preferable to the bustling, vividly painted horror that stretched out before him. This place was loud. Full of life, yet lifeless all the same. Metal and stone that reeked of urine. Blazing lights that seared into the skull around every corner. Pulsing vibrations claimed the air, prickling over the skin and numbing the mind.

"It is certainly... something," a dissonant voice echoed in his thoughts. A spectral companion, now a stowaway in his body. His accomplice.

"It nauseates me," Morgan growled.

A passerby collided with his shoulder. Pain lanced down his arm where the rune he had carved into his flesh still healed. His silver eyes danced with fury, violet light overtaking the irises.

"Best not to draw attention to us, my lord."

His ire flickered out with the magic in his eyes as the one who had bumped him bolted away in terror. He assessed the stranger's attire as they ran, low-hanging trousers and an ill-fitted cloak of vibrant colors. With another glint of violet, his mirage of outdated clothing shifted to mirror the ragged ensemble. "Hmm." He glanced down at himself. "I think not."

"Most certainly not."

"Is that amusement I sense in you, Daffyd?" He prowled further along a raised side path for pedestrians as mechanical transports in every shape and color roared down the main road.

"Forgive me. It has been too long since I was able to wear naught but the tattered armor I fell in."

"I share your pain, old friend. Though at least you bore clothes in *your* death," Morgan said, turning a corner to escape the wailing beats of the street behind him. "While my glamour may sheath my nakedness, it does nothing to repel this chill in the air."

"As I said, my lord, you were clothed."

"Yes, yes," Morgan snapped, "but to what end if I was to be left forgotten for seventeen centuries? There was enough magic within my tomb to preserve my body while my garments rotted to nothing? Careless spellwork."

A group of disorderly youths walked along the path opposite him, shouting obscenities into the masses. He eyed the man who seemed to be spurring them on where he stood at the center of the crowd, wearing a simple, white shirt with sleeves no longer than his biceps and a plunging neckline. Morgan's sagging wrap was whisked away, replaced in an instant with the form-fitting top.

"Oh." He marveled at his arms and chest, revealing a large portion of the coiling black markings that cascaded from his neck and down his right arm. "I quite enjoy that."

"An improvement to be sure."

A sharp crack suddenly filled the air from a nearby alley. People ran, screaming. Curiosity pulled at Morgan, a hook behind his navel, drawing him to the source of chaos.

"My lord..."

"Be still, Daffyd," he whispered, creeping into the dark passage. "I wish to know what fuels the nightmares of these peasants. It may be of use."

Panicked voices echoed off the stone walls.

"I got nothin', man! I swear!" a trembling figure screamed from the ground, shielding their face with their arms. "Please! Just let my brother go! He's just a kid!"

A smaller shadow cowered against the wall behind the man on the ground. A muscled form stood above them, arm outstretched, bearing a long glint of iron. The assailant bore hints of light embedded in their flesh. Lines of red glowed beneath their eyes. Polished metal wrapped their jaw, neck, and hands as if opting for plate armor instead of skin.

"You know what we do with piss that can't pay the toll?" the hulking thug growled. "We take it out of your cold, dead corpse."

"You might've just said 'corpse,'" Morgan droned, causing the man to whip around, aiming his weapon at him. "Rather redundant, your threat."

"The fuck?" the metal-plated man spat. "What kinda dit ass moron are you? This is Reaper business!"

"Reaper..." Morgan muttered, thumbing his lower lip. "A servant of Arawn? You? Unlikely, considering he seems to have abandoned this world along with the rest."

"I believe it to be a moniker, my lord, nothing more."

"Ah," Morgan mused. "A farce to instill terror. How quaint."

"What are you even sayin'?" The man stalked forward, brandishing his iron stick. "You slip out of the CD Asylum, bro? Who even *talks* like that?"

"The iron simpleton has a point, Lord Morgan. Your speech is likely to draw attention, even with your alter rune cloaking your identity."

"Dude, get out of here!" The man on the ground scrambled to his feet, moving to shield his brother. "He's a Reaper! They don't listen to reason—they just kill!"

Morgan pressed his lips together, wholly unbothered by the warning. His eyes shimmered violet. Light flared from the inside of his left bicep, a diamond with a single line through it, shining where he had carved the spellwork necessary to escape his prison—the spell hiding away his true name and nature.

"What the shit are you, man?! You one of those OC freaks?!" the Reaper roared. "Oh, this night just got *so* luxe! I'm gonna be a *legend*, takin' out one of you Well-suckers!"

"The Well? They know of the Well?"

"Seems nothing is secret in this shithole," Morgan hissed—his voice shifting, hiding away his dialect as his rune's power increased, breathing in the surrounding culture. "Even Avalon."

The Reaper cackled through the alley, turning back to the young men behind him. "I'm almost tempted to tell you worthless fucks to scramble. Don't need your chips and comms anymore when I got this little trophy to take back to HQ. But I'd get an ass kickin' if I let a mark get away. Sit tight." He pulled back something at the end of his weapon with a click, staring Morgan down. Another crack echoed off the walls.

Morgan cocked his head, eyes aglow. He held an arm out, examining the small piece of metal the device had released where it hung in the space. "Huh."

"Cowardly," Daffyd huffed. *"No elegance nor skill required."*

"Sure," Morgan whispered, ignoring the panic on the Reaper's face. "But it does give an advantage in battle, you gotta admit."

"I don't care for this new tone of yours. Change it back."

Morgan snickered, plucking the projectile from the air.

"Wh-What the *fuck?!"* the brute roared, taking his weapon in both hands. "DIE, YOU *FREAK!"*

Morgan's attention snapped back to the Reaper as a hail of metal filled the space, every single attack halted midair. A grin tugged at the corner of his lips. His brows descended, taunting his would-be killer. "A Reaper, *are you?"* He wafted his hand, spinning every single projectile to face the other direction. "It wouldn't be the first time I've thwarted death."

The man backed away, clicking the weapon in his hand over and again, but it would respond no more.

"And it won't be the last." With a flick of his finger, Morgan sent the metal fragments flying, ripping the other man's body to shreds with a force that tore right through his metal-plated flesh.

The Reaper's eyes grew wide. He let out a pained groan, dropping to his knees. "F-Fuck..." The man fell face-first to the ground, blood soaking the black stone where he lay.

The pair of men against the wall stared at Morgan, faces filled with horror and uncertainty as their eyes flitted between him and their assailant's body.

"W-What do you want?" The older man choked, wrapping his arms around his brother.

Morgan considered them briefly before dropping to the balls of his feet to retrieve the Reaper's armament, lifting it curiously to his face. "What's this called?"

"Um..." the younger man said, "that's a gun."

"A gun..." Morgan whispered, fiddling with a cylinder that spun when prodded.

"It's... It's a revolver," the older man sputtered, standing. "How do you not know what a gun is? Nearly everyone in Etna is packing."

"Not from around here," Morgan droned, looking over the corpse.

The Reaper wore a black, leather sort of surcoat. It was short and made of too little material to accomplish much in the way of protection, ending at the man's ribcage. Feeling the dank air of the alley on his naked body, Morgan leaned over, shucking the coat from the man's limp form. With a hint of violet, the leather shimmered. The holes left by Morgan's assault wove themselves together. The bloodstains vanished.

Morgan swung the coat over his shoulders, blocking out the cold. He was drowning in it, enveloped in a garment made to fit a man three times his size. Slowly, the leather began to shrink, smaller and smaller, until it was nearly skintight on his lithe form.

"Now, that looks imposing, my lord."

"I like it," Morgan mused, admiring himself. "Could do with a bigger collar. Maybe a bit of silver embellishment."

"Wow..." the young man whispered. "That is so *cool!*"

"Hush, Jordy," the older one hissed, throwing an arm out to shield his little brother. "He's a *witch*. They're just as bad as Reapers. Maybe worse."

"You've met other witches, then?" Morgan shot him a glance.

The man swallowed nervously. "N-No. They keep to themselves."

"Then how do you know what they're like?" Morgan raised a single brow, smiling.

"You hear stuff." The man shrugged, eyeing the exit to the alleyway. "They only look out for themselves. Esotech are the ones that use magic for commons like us. Witches want nothing to do with the outside world after the war."

Morgan huffed a laugh, tucking the revolver into his pocket. "All this time and they still haven't learned a damn thing." He took a step deeper into the alley, making for the next street.

The older brother inhaled sharply, pulling his sibling back toward the wall.

Morgan sighed, stopping in his tracks. "If I wanted you dead, I would've sent one of those projectiles your way."

The grown man blew a breath through his lips, nodding. "Bullets."

Morgan lifted his brows in question.

"That's what they're called. The things that come out of a gun. Bullets." The man relaxed slightly, and a small laugh escaped his lungs. "Where exactly are you from that doesn't know these things? Sounds like a dream."

The threads of Morgan's lost memory danced through his thoughts. A sudden echo of laughter. A cry of rage followed by blistering heat and the smell of burnt flesh. An embrace, warm and comforting.

Longing sparked his chest.

"What... was that, my lord?"

Morgan shook the thoughts from his head, frustrated at his moment of weakness and having forgotten that his mind was a shared space for the time being. "A dream. Nothing but a dream."

"O-kay..." The man eyed him warily.

Morgan cleared his throat, striding away from the pair to leave. He reached the edge of the alley, the bustle of the city street only a few steps ahead.

"Hey!" The younger man, Jordy, called after him. "What's your name?"

Morgan paused. He clenched his fists, staring out into the street. "My name..." He looked up to the sky, stars hidden behind clouds and the light of the city.

"You mustn't speak that name anymore, my lord. Not here. Not now."

Morgan closed his eyes. A raindrop hit his cheek. "Etna..."

"Lord Morgan?"

"Forever to live in its shadow, even now..." Morgan turned back to the men in the alley as the rain began to fall in waves. "My name is Fell," he shouted. "Morgan Fell."

We come now to the very first tale the world was ever told about our heroes.

I struggled with what I could share about Aaron and Morgan prior to Sapphire's release, but desperately wanted to give a glimpse into their story. The result still makes me smile.

A holiday tale that tells of an almost. A chance passing in the night that may or may not have contributed to all that was to come.

This short was released on December 21st, 2023

A Sapphire Solstice

12.21.202 UI

For nearly two centuries, for just one week at the end of every year, the neon city of Etna was cast in a cozy blanket of glittering, white snow as the towering climate generators that lined the outer wall went into the winter cycle. The spectrum of lights that painted every stone façade shifted to tones of emerald and crimson, and the faces of the citizens who walked the streets held subtle glints of joy that rarely graced the masses. For unto the end of the world did mankind cling to that everlasting hope that sprang from the changing of the season—the Solstice.

That hope would not be afforded to the Lynxes of the North District this night, however, hiding away in an old hatchery along the coast that had become nothing more than a front for manufacturing stardust; Etna City's fastest route to rock bottom. The gang had been struggling for a foothold in the streets against the ever-present Reapers, until Darren Mulvaney—a would-be crime lord hoisted up on broken promises and more debt than the corrupt Ministers of the city held combined—brokered a deal with them to run his drug op. An operation that stoked fury within one of the true crime lords of Etna, Ventnor Caine.

And thus, Morgan Fell found himself running from the dank air of the hatchery in the dead of night, away from the smell of rotten fish and the metallic tang of chemicals.

"GET HIM!" a burly, shirtless Lynx yelled, barreling across the flimsy, wooden planks as three other thugs panted behind him.

Morgan screeched to a halt at the entrance, a wicked grin on his lips as he whirled back. "Sorry, boys." His eyes flashed violet as he raised both hands, lifting the men from their feet into the air. "No witnesses and all that." With clenched fists, he dragged them all to the ground, rattling the floorboards and filling the room with pained groans. "Be grateful this is the face you get to remember in the dark."

With a wink, he kicked off the wood beneath his feet, propelling himself backward through the door. He spiraled through the air toward the street, jet-black hair vanishing against the night sky as he reached for the magic that now canvassed the building he'd left behind. His eyes blazed, he snapped his fingers, and as his feet met the asphalt, the hatchery was engulfed in blistering flames. In mere seconds, the fire found the catalysts that were the many components of stardust, and the air ignited.

Morgan averted his eyes, holding up a faint shield of violet light as he reached for his pocket. "Phase two complete," he growled into his phone.

"I'll say," his snarky apprentice shot back. "Get a move on to phase three before I have to deal with ECPD already!"

"Yeah, yeah," Morgan snickered, trotting across the street to straddle his flashy, black and chrome motorcycle—a custom ordered Delubrexa PT400. With a flick at his screen, the call transferred to the vehicle's built-in radio. "You sure you don't wanna join me for a drink at The Spire, Daph? I hear Benny's got candied Snow Roses on the bar tonight. You could make a *wish*."

Daphne blew a raspberry over the line. "You know damn well they're not the real thing."

"Aww, come on," Morgan teased, peeling out onto the road. "Where's your holiday spirit?"

"Why do you get so gooey over Solstice?" Daphne asked, laughing. "Any other day you're as callous as they come. Jingle bells and candy canes hit and bam—you're like Santa Claus with a hatchet."

"You know there's an actual evil Santa Claus, right? People were obsessed with him a few centuries ago. So many gory flicks on the archives."

"It genuinely terrifies me how little you know of old pop culture until it comes to Santa Claus."

Morgan's laugh was audible above the roar of his engine. "Hey, I've been on the guy's naughty list for ages, right? He's gotta be a witch. Better to know my enemy in case his story has some truth to it too."

"Battle strategy? That's your excuse?" Daphne chuckled. "Honestly, I'd pay a fortune to see that fight go down."

"You never know!" Morgan snickered, disappearing into the city streets as the fires behind him became nothing but a distant glow in the night.

"Forget it, Lex!" Aaron hissed, dropping his hushed tone now that they were out of earshot of the Eastside Meadows staff as they stepped out into the brisk night air. "I'm not going anywhere within a five-mile radius of that creep!"

Lexi trotted along after him as they paced the sidewalk to Aaron's tiny, red Canaba sport, her rose-gold hair flying wildly in the bitter wind. "We don't even know he's there! We've been planning this for *weeks*, Aaron! We are not going to let that dit-wad, Connor Daniels, spoil our traditional night out with Dani and the gang!"

Aaron huffed, rolling his bright, blue eyes at her as he dropped into the driver's seat while she leapt in beside him. "He's already done that. Even if he's not there, I'll be looking over my shoulder all night, worried he might show. I can't take that. Not tonight." He clenched his eyes shut, gripping the steering wheel.

Solstice was once the most wonderful time of Aaron Jones's life. It was the time that his mom got a paid holiday from work. It was when Grams would fill her cozy little apartment with cheer and they would spend magical nights in the courtyard outside, singing carols over cups of cocoa around a towering tree. Grams tried so very hard for two years after his mother's accident to keep that cheer alive, but it was never the same, and Aaron wasn't in a place to appreciate what he had left before even that was ripped away from him.

"Okay," Lexi said softly, reaching out to grasp his arm. "You're right. I can't put you through that. I'll message Dani and see if she can get us in anywhere else. Other side of the city if we have to, but we're not spending the night sulking, deal?"

Aaron nodded gently when a notice blared in the left side of his vision.

ATTN: ALL AVAILABLE OFFICERS. EXPLOSION REPORTED. ND S1H. REPORT. ALL AVAILABLE OFFICERS.

He tapped three times at his left temple to silence the alert with a growl.

"What?" Lexi snapped. "Don't you dare, Jones. Not tonight. You're off duty. Doctor's orders."

Aaron shook his head with a small smile. "I'm not. Just an explosion, not a rift. Probably gang bullshit."

"I don't care if a rift opens on every block in Etna, mister," she chided, "you're drinking and dancing with your girls tonight, and that's that."

"Dancing?" Aaron looked at her in horror. "I never agreed to dancing! Where are we going?"

Lexi's lips curved up with a devious glint in her eye. "Dani reached out to Benny, and tonight he's working at—you will not believe it—the place our heartthrob, bad boy witch first stole our hearts—"

"No *way*."

"Oh yeah! We're going to *The Spire*, Jones!"

***

Morgan pushed past the crowds lining the sidewalk, earning shouts of annoyance and several insults that were cut short as people caught sight of his face. His reputation certainly had its uses. The bouncer made to step in front of him with a hand held out in rebuke, but immediately stepped aside, choking on his words. "S–Sorry, Mister Fell. Your host is waiting for you in the VIP lounge. You can go right up."

Morgan spared him a glance, nodded in thanks, and waved the personal chip embedded in his right palm over a scanner in the doorframe. He tapped the pad below, tipping the man a few thousand credits as he stepped into the pulsing atmosphere of The Spire. "Happy Solstice."

"Th-Thank you, Mister Fell! You too!" the man sputtered after him.

A vibrant spectacle of flashing lights and dazzling bodies—some clothed and others toying with the lines that defined nudity—spread out across the holographic dance floor. Projected snowflakes fell from the ceiling in a cascade of sparkling white and blue. A melodic trance filled the space like an electric siren song, sweeping away the senses with every vibration. Through the revelers and the swell of lights, Morgan caught the eye of the bartender.

Benny was an attractive man with brown hair that ran to his chiseled jaw. His pearl skin was painted with highlights to accent his sharp cheekbones and his eyes were dark with mascara. Morgan offered a single nod that Benny returned, before turning toward the staircase in the far corner of the room.

Two muscled men who seemed near bursting free of their designer suits exchanged a glance at Morgan's approach, nodded, and stepped away from one another to allow him access. The one on the left reached for his temple with a series of taps as the one on the right stared Morgan down.

A grin tugged at the corner of Morgan's lips, and his eyes flashed violet. "Take a walk. Pretend you're right where you're expected to be," he growled, turning to the second bodyguard. "Both of you."

The men's faces glazed over in an instant. They moved autonomously through the shadows of the club, around a corner, and out the back door. Morgan wafted up the carpeted staircase to the high balcony overlooking the dance floor. A man of Ventnor Caine's repute should have known better than to have his men posted where he couldn't keep eyes on them, but then, men of his repute so often grew complacent, certain of the terror their very names provided.

A glass door slid aside with a gentle hiss, and an icy voice called in greeting, "Mister *Fell*. Please, join me for a drink, won't you?"

Morgan inclined his head to the man where he sat on a plush, velvet sofa. Caine was what mobster flicks of old were made of—a pinstripe suit, slicked back hair and a scarred lip, filling the room with smoke from the cigar between his fingers. His eyes literally glowed with rings of yellow, courtesy of the implants that were little more than intimidation factor according to Daphne's intel.

Sitting opposite the man over a neon-lit coffee table, Morgan spread his arms across the back of the sofa and crossed one leg over the other as Caine slid a whiskey glass toward him. He leaned forward to snatch it up, and as his fingers touched the cold glass, his eyes glistened for the briefest of moments while Caine was distracted by his comm. He took a generous sip of the drink, leaning back.

"Mighty fine work for a merc, I must say," Caine rasped, puffing his cigar. "I don't suppose I might interest you in a more... *permanent* relationship?"

Morgan snickered into his drink. "Sorry, Caine. I have commitment issues."

"Ah, of course." Caine chuckled darkly. "Don't all men like you? Dark and mysterious, no strings. And what could I possibly offer the infamous Morgan Fell that he doesn't already have?"

"You'd be surprised," Morgan laughed. "But there's little this city can keep out of my grasp when I want it."

Caine hummed, nodding his head. "I believe that. That is exactly why I'm offering you this one-time deal, Morgan. I know all too well about your quarrel with Esotech. I know you prefer your solitude and your secrecy above all else. You're a lone agent—a free man with an axe to grind against the most powerful force in this city." Caine leaned back, extending an arm in welcome. "Come work with me. With your abilities and my connections, we could run Etna. You wouldn't need to hide yourself away. You could take every pound of flesh you crave, and all I would ask in return is your loyalty. You can't say our interests aren't aligned, not after tonight."

Morgan smiled wickedly, shaking his head. "You see, that's the thing everyone gets wrong about me. You all assume I hide for my own safety. You all think that I'm the one that's in danger every time I show my face for the things I've done."

Morgan lifted his head to meet the man's eyes. "I work alone because *you're* the ones that should be afraid."

Caine barked a laugh. "Such *spirit!* It's almost as if you believe your own bravado! It's magnificent!" The man grinned, nodding to the drink in Morgan's hand. "Please remember, I did extend my hand in friendship, but if you aren't on my leash, I can't have a wildfire like you blazing across my city. It's bad for business, you see. In payment for your fine work, I will ensure that your death is painless, however."

Morgan rolled his head back with a cackle. "Speaking of bravado."

"Oh, no, my boy," Caine said sadly. "I'm afraid you'll find that my subtle blend of iron and Rohypnol in your drink has left you without your magic and, very soon, without your wits. A true shame to have to do away with such a pretty face, but a man in my position can't afford to get distracted by shiny th—" His monologue was cut short, a shocked expression blossoming across his face with a grunt.

"This drink?" Morgan snickered, his hand empty as he waved toward the coffee table. The glass sat exactly where Caine had left it, its contents untouched.

"Wh—*How?*" the man hissed through gritted teeth as blood stained the white shirt beneath his suit jacket.

Morgan leaned forward, resting his elbows on his knees. "It never fails to amaze me how little people know of magic. They want the benefits but know absolutely nothing of its potential. The great Ventnor Caine, undone by single glamour... and a *couch spring.*"

The man's eyes bulged as another piece of metal pierced his back.

"Two couch springs."

"You're... a walking corpse," Caine spat. "My people are everywhere. I am one member of my ring. You took out... a scab in that hatchery. *This...* you have *no* idea—"

"Your ring is dead." Morgan shrugged, sinking back into the couch. "Took care of 'em three days ago."

Caine laughed, coating his lower lip in blood. "Bullshit. I apprised them of your progress twenty minutes ago."

"Oh, right," Morgan said. "My cipher says you're quite the chatterbox. Knew you had a contingency in place when I walked in. Didn't think it would be so *basic*, though."

Caine let out an elongated growl as another spring ripped into him. "My men won't let you leave. You'll... have the ECPD all over you. You're *fucked!*"

Morgan laughed, rising to his feet. "Your men are off to live their lives. As soon as they regain their senses, they'll find a very generous severance package waiting for them—courtesy of the benevolent Ventnor Caine before he disappears into retirement."

Caine roared, rooted to the couch as blood spattered down his front. "You don't know what... you're doing, Fell! You're giving up *Olympus* here! I could make you a GOD!"

"Met the gods." Morgan stopped on his way through the door, glancing over his shoulder at the man with a bored look. "Wasn't impressed. My regards to Mulvaney and his thugs." With a jut of his head, a torrent of springs shredded Caine's back, red dripping from the corner of his mouth to drench his suit, and his head dropped to one side.

Morgan trotted back down onto the dance floor, closing the access door to the VIP balcony with a tilt of his head and sealing it with a glint of violet. He shot Daphne a short message to confirm his kill, then paced across the pulsing floor to an open seat at the bar.

"Scotch on the rocks with a twist?" Benny asked, leaning over the counter with a smirk.

"Make it double, Benny." Morgan smiled brightly. "The city has reason to celebrate tonight."

"Aye, mighty strange thing, that." Benny nodded with feigned morosity. "An entire crime syndicate just packing it in. I take it you left my lounge intact?"

Morgan grinned, taking the glass in earnest this time as it was handed to him. "You're gonna need a new couch."

Benny jerked back with furrowed brows.

"I had to keep things quiet," Morgan said, giving an innocent shrug. "I improvised."

Benny chuckled lightly as a vase of glimmering, blue flowers on the back counter caught Morgan's attention. "Ah," the bartender breathed. "You spotted my Solstice special, I see. Care to make a wish, Fell?"

Morgan laughed, shaking his head. "First of all, those aren't the genuine article, or you wouldn't be selling them at three hundred creds a pop."

"*Dude!*" Benny hissed. "Don't go spilling the beans on my money maker!"

"Second of all," Morgan continued with a grin, "I don't do wishes. If I need something, I make it happen. You put all your hopes and dreams out there, and you never know who might come calling to take advantage."

Benny eyed him with a thoughtful smirk before pacing to the back bar. He snatched up a single blue flower from the vase, its petals rose-like in form but lacking the distinctive heart shape of a true Snow Rose, and passed it across the counter to Morgan. "On the house. Go on. I *dare* you."

Morgan took the flower gingerly between his fingers, recalling the last time he'd looked upon the real thing lifetimes past—a world he hardly remembered. A sudden ache filled his chest. He cast a cautious glance around the room, turning away from the onlookers he usually drew in public, and his eyes glowed violet. Life shuddered through the plant beneath the dusting of sugar coating the petals. The deep, blue dye that soaked the plant shimmered away, a soft powder-blue and white taking its place. The edges of the petals curled inward and back out, morphing before their eyes to take the heart shape in Morgan's mind. With a wicked grin, he passed the flower back to Benny.

"Okay, wow." Benny stared in wonder at the Snow Rose in his hand. "It's *beautiful*, Morgan, but... I gotta say, I'm with you on the whole wishes thing. Not really my style."

Morgan snickered, downing the last of his drink. "Alright, then. It's Solstice. Everyone deserves a little magic this time of year. Pass it off to someone who really needs it. Someone with enough heart to wish this whole damn city right."

The frigid air nipped at Aaron's knuckles as he stood in the alley of The Spire with Lexi, Dani and two other girls from Dani's salon. Dani was a vision, sporting hot-rod red locks that made her look like the rockstar she was on the inside, and a gold sequin jacket over her copper skin. Tasha was just as gorgeous, tall and dark-skinned with flowing extensions of vibrant reds and greens to show her holiday spirit. Mira was petite, done up in dark makeup to contrast her pale complexion, and while she was beautiful, she possessed an air a bit more extreme than even Lexi's. It was the sort that told anyone that she would kick their ass just for looking at her the wrong way.

Lexi laughed as she waved her cigarette through the air, the smell and the alcohol in Aaron's veins tempting him to snatch it away to take a hit. He pushed aside the sudden urge and laughed along with the others, shivering in the cold.

"Sooo, Jonesy?" Dani cooed, staring at him from where she leaned against the brick wall. "See anything you like in there?"

"Huh, what?" Aaron sputtered as all eyes turned to him.

"Oh, don't even start with that, Dani baby," Lexi said, giggling. "There's only one man in this city capable of pulling this one out of the depths of his own head on a night like this."

"Oh?" Tasha mused. "Who might *that* be?"

"Ugh, why, Lex? *Why?*" Aaron forgot the cold as his face flushed.

"Come on, then," Mira teased. "Who on earth could make *Aaron Jones* blush like *that?*"

"I hate all of you," Aaron growled.

"Why, the one and only—"

"Alexandra—"

"The gorgeous, the mysterious and broody—"

"I swear on the wheels of my mother's bed—"

"*Morgan Fell.*"

All of the girls swiveled their heads to Aaron with tight-lipped smiles, squealing with drunken delight. Aaron ran a palm down his face defeatedly. "It's your fault. You pointed the handsome bastard out to me. Not like any one of you would kick him out of bed."

"Except," Tasha shook her head with a smirk, "none of *us* would have a shot."

"Wh-What are you talking about?" Aaron stared at her in disbelief. "You're all freaking *gorgeous*. He'd be stupid not to look at you twice."

"Oh, I have no doubt he could appreciate our beauty," Dani snickered. "But he'd never crawl into bed with us."

"What?" Aaron asked, completely lost.

"Honey," Lexi patted his shoulder with a sad look. "He's *gay*."

"Wh-*WHAT?*" Aaron gasped. "How do you even know that? You and I have had *countless* conversations about him, and you're just now telling me this?!"

Lexi shot him a dumbfounded look before breaking into a laugh so hard that she had to balance herself on his arm. "I thought you *knew*, dummy! Gods, the way you drool over him sometimes, I figured there was no way you couldn't!"

Aaron groaned in his throat, but a smile tugged at his lips. That was fair. Only with a bit of inebriation would he ever admit it, but it was fair. Not that this revelation would ever, in any way make his fever dreams over a man he had only ever seen on wanted posters and the five o'clock news any more real. "I'm ready for another drink. You good?"

"Yeah," Lexi panted, still laughing as she snuffed her cigarette out with her heel. "Yeah let's—" The roar of a motorcycle engine cut the air as a shadow darkened the alley for the whisper of an instant.

"Who the fuck drives a bike during the winter cycle?" Mira yelled after the shadow that was no doubt already on the other side of the city with the speed they had passed them at.

Aaron shot Lexi a look of awe that she returned before staring back out to the street.

Waving the other girls off, he sulked toward the bar as they flocked to one of the men in nothing but tight, shimmering pants who sold colorful shots from a serving tray. He leaned over the counter, waiting for Benny to notice him as his thoughts trailed off at the enchanting beat of the club.

Morgan Fell.

It was at this very counter that Aaron had first seen the man. At least, he very much believed it had been the same man. He was caught on the CCTV of The Spire's security during a gruesome investigation involving a serial killer that specifically targeted dance clubs. Magically—whether metaphorical or otherwise—the killer was never seen again after that night, and the young man he was last seen with was never identified, a face too blurry for even top-of-the-line cameras to catch.

The clatter of ice on glass snapped Aaron back to the present, and he looked up to see Benny smiling over him as he shoved a crystal blue drink in his direction before placing the most beautiful rose Aaron had ever seen on top, dusted with glittering sugar.

"Whoa, too rich for my blood, Benjamin," Aaron chuckled. "I just need a beer."

"It's paid for." Benny shot him a wink. "Secret admirer."

Aaron whipped his head around, scanning the bar and the dance floor beyond. "Who?"

"Nah, he had to jet." Benny shrugged, pouting. "Tried to get him to leave you his line, but he's a stubborn thing. It's a shame, really. Together, you boys would be a sight this city would never forget."

"This secret, stubborn, perfect man of mine have a name?" Aaron scoffed, plucking the rose from his drink.

"I reckon he has a few, guy like that, and he'd kill me right and proper if I gave you any of them against his wishes." Benny laughed. "Speaking of wishes, you be careful with that rose. Coming from *him*, during *Solstice*? I wouldn't doubt the legends."

Benny nodded once, moving away to libate the masses as Aaron twirled the marvelous flower between his fingers.

"Legends, huh?" Aaron whispered, entranced by the way the petals shimmered in the many surrounding lights. The pulsing music of the club faded into a dull roar in his ears as a sensation of utmost serenity overtook his senses. In his peace, the faces of the ones he cherished most crossed his mind. His mother where she lay in the home he'd left hours ago. Lexi, smiling brightly somewhere in the room behind him. His beloved Grams, wherever she may be, watching over him from afar.

A strange scent filled his nose suddenly, though not the scent of the flower in his grasp. It was energy and comfort. Electricity and earth.

It was leather and lightning.

I wish...

The First Annual All Hallows' Eve Party at the newly established, hottest club in the city, The Majesty…

…interrupted.

I had so much fun writing this Halloween short. A nod to my favorite comic book heroes, a rift like the boys have never experienced, and a heartwarming ending even I wasn't expecting.

This short was released on October 31st, 2024

A Night at Cosmic Castle

10.31.203 UI

Betwixt the vibrant summer sun and chill of winter's breath, a night of fun and trickery, beyond even the veil of death. Unto the end of time, that age-old celebration stood, a testament to man's fascination with the wild and strange. And the neon city did love its parties, it was fact, and would never change.

"Baby, I am fully supportive of your nerdy, adorable little heart, you know that," Morgan groaned from the bathroom, messing with a strange circlet of banded silver wrapped around his head, "but getting me to play a video game is one thing. Now you have me dressing like a cartoon character?"

"*Comic book* character, babe!" Aaron shouted from the bedroom. "These characters are legendary! They've been around for *hundreds* of years!"

Morgan eyed the tattered red cloak he'd hung on the door, snapping the stretchy black material that covered his chest against his skin to make certain he wasn't dreaming.

"*We're* legendary. Actual legends. What do these guys have on us?"

"Okay, so..." Aaron appeared in the doorway, covered in tight-fitted black and purple armor that made him look like knight from outer space. "...my character is the royal offspring of two alien races that have been at war for like... forever—"

Sucking his bottom lip between his teeth, Morgan let his eyes glaze over as he basked in the crazed, passionate glow on his boyfriend's face while he rambled off his comic book knowledge. Honestly, anything that made Aaron positively giddy was worth doing. He'd happily parade himself out on the street wearing a fluffy pink dress while holding a magic wand if it got the same reaction.

"—well, your character, who is the son of probably the strongest witch in the universe, gets teamed up with him and they fall in love. Eventually they even get married and rule the cosmos together. They're the perfect costumes for us, I promise."

"*You're* perfect," Morgan swooned, practically blinking cartoon hearts out of his eyes.

"And you heard absolutely nothing I said, did you?" Aaron chuckled, leaning in to peck his lips.

Morgan shrugged innocently, snatching his cloak off the door. "Doesn't matter. I'm convinced. Whatever makes my boyfriend happy."

"A *little* interest would make your boyfriend happy." Aaron crossed his arms over his chest, shaking his head with a grin.

"Aaron, I'm wearing elastane on my entire body." Morgan rolled his eyes, slipping the cloak over his head to rest on his shoulders. "You can see *everything*. You're happy."

Those blue eyes instantly flicked down to Morgan's crotch. Aaron pursed his lips to one side of his face. "I don't like it. Lose the cape."

"No!" Morgan whined, pulling the fabric to his chest possessively. "It's my favorite part. *My cape.*"

"Well, it's blocking my view of *my* favorite part," Aaron laughed, poking him in his sides. "So, absorb my nerdy ravings or lose the cape and show me that ass!"

Morgan giggled uncontrollably as he backed into the counter, fighting off his boyfriend's attempt to tickle him senseless when Daphne shouted from the hall, "You two ready?! The club is packed and the party's already started!"

"I'm being attacked by a horny emperor from outer space!" Morgan yelled through fits of laughter, swatting at Aaron's hands. "Help!"

"Nope!" Daphne cackled, quickly walking away. "I'm out! See you downstairs!"

Aaron rolled his head back with a chuckle before moving closer, pinning Morgan between the counter and his thighs. He brushed a strand of hair off the circlet on Morgan's head, then wrapped a hand around the back of his neck. "We should probably get a move on, huh?"

"I want to say no," Morgan whispered against his lips as he leaned in, "but if I take this outfit off, I am *not* putting it back on."

A small whimper of protest left Aaron's throat as Morgan kissed him, tugging at his bottom lip with his teeth when he pulled away.

Morgan snickered, stealing another chaste kiss. "Come on, space man. We can make hot intergalactic alien-witch love after the party."

The Majesty, Morgan's ballroom venue turned nightclub, was packed from corner to corner. Its usual purple and blue ambiance had been set aside in favor of orange, green and yellow. Where holographic dancers normally stood on raised platforms along the walls, spooky faces now pulsed in time with the beat, grinning and laughing from above. While opening night just a couple weeks prior had been a sensation, boasting one of the biggest turnouts in the city, those numbers were now put to shame.

Heads turned the moment Aaron and Morgan stepped into the room. It was difficult to say if their costumes drew the attention—considering Aaron had asked for a glamour to turn his skin green and give him a set of dragon-like wings before leaving the Manor—or if, like any other night they arrived hand in hand, people simply recognized them instantly: Etna city's bad boy witch and his ex-cop turned mercenary, out living it up in their own club.

"Whoa, fellas!" the DJ shouted over the music, pointing their way from the stage. "Morgan, your man's lookin' a little *green!* He jelly everyone's staring, or you two start the party early?"

"Aaand, he's fired," Morgan groaned loudly, rolling his eyes. He would never fire Gio. The guy was magic in the sound booth. Literally.

"The city would *riot!*" a slightly slurred shout came from the direction of the bar. Flaming red locks hung over a gold tiara, framing a mischievous grin as Gwen bounced her way over, done up in a gorgeous pink and white ball gown. She held out two plastic cups as he approached. "Took you two long enough!" She looked Aaron up and down with a snort of laughter. "You are *such* a dork."

"Hey," Morgan pouted, pulling Aaron against his side. "That's *my* dork you're talking to."

"Hate you both," Aaron grumbled before taking a swig from the cup Gwen offered. "At least I stepped out of my comfort zone, *princess*."

"This was *never* my comfort zone, and you know it," Gwen said with a smirk.

Lance came up from behind her, wrapping his arms around her waist and wearing what Morgan pegged for the armor he wore the night he arrived in Etna. The costume was almost identical, apart from the finery that had been changed to a pristine white fabric with gold embroidery.

"Speaking of comfort zones," Morgan muttered, hiding a grin behind his glass. Something offensively sweet poured over his tongue, tasting of candy and vodka. "And now I have to fire the bartender too," he choked, screwing up his face with disgust. "What is this piss?"

Gwen chuckled, waving them toward the bar. "I think that's the poison apple punch."

Morgan's brow furrowed as they followed. "Why are we poisoning our guests? Why are we poisoning *me?*"

"It's just a themed drink, sweetheart," Aaron laughed, knocking back the rest of his drink with a gulp. "It's not actually poisoned."

"I don't know how true that is," Morgan droned, holding out his cup for Aaron, begging him to save him from having to drink the rest.

Aaron took the drink, shaking his head as he scanned the night's menu, a glowing board lit with a black light. "I think he'll take a—"

The bartender slid a whiskey glass across the counter, filled with a caramel-colored liquid and decorated with a cinnamon stick and an orange curl. "I gotcha, boss."

Morgan squinted at the man, covered with paint to look like a very sparkly skeleton wearing a lopsided top hat. "Shane?"

Shane shot him a wink, pushing the drink closer. "Spiced bourbon, tested it myself."

"Why are you working the bar?" Morgan asked, taking a curious sip of the drink. Warmth slid down his throat, making his tummy tingle and his lips curve with satisfaction.

"Eh, never been big on All Hallows' Eve," Shane said with a shrug. "Figured I'd give Percy a break."

"Where *is* Percy?" Aaron mused, scanning the crowd.

"Out on the dance floor with Lucas, Daphne and Frey," Gwen hummed, smiling into her glass. "Haven't seen him since he got here."

"Lucas showed?" Morgan's brows raised.

"You invited him, babe," Aaron said with a chuckle. "The guy has been your biggest fan since the wastes. Of course, he showed."

"He borrowed Bryn's armor." Lance jutted his chin toward the middle of the club. "No idea how they're dancing in the stuff. I just hope they don't step on anyone's toes."

"No Wain?" Morgan sighed, watching his friends dance.

"Oh, he's handling security, also wearing his armor," Gwen laughed airily, pointing up to the balcony. "I think he feels more at home than he has all month."

Morgan followed her finger, catching the eye of the hulking man in white and silver armor above. Gawain nodded once with a grin and a wave before stalking along the balcony with his arms crossed.

Aaron bumped Morgan's shoulder with his. "Hey, sexy, wanna dance?"

"Do your dances resemble our Earth dances, Mister alien?" Morgan deadpanned, taking another sip of his drink.

"He grew up on Earth, you butthole," Aaron chuckled, giving him a gentle shove. "So, yes."

Quickly finishing his drink, Morgan dropped his glass on the bar counter, taking Aaron's hand when everyone around him reached for their temples.

"Oh, fuck," Aaron groaned.

"On All Hallows' Eve?" Gwen sighed, slumping back against the bar. "Come *on*."

Morgan didn't need to ask. He'd left his phone at the Manor, having nowhere on his person to store it comfortably. As those among their friends with implants had received an alert but the club hadn't, it could only mean that Daphne's recently installed system to detect rifts throughout the city had gone off.

"Where is it?" Morgan asked, frowning.

"West District," Daphne called across the floor suddenly, pushing past clubgoers to reach them. Her own costume mirrored Shane's, embellished with shimmering yellow jewels over her face paint and her hair pulled up in a gold crown. "It's... oh, that's spooky."

"Oh, you've gotta be joking," Aaron laughed, shaking his head. "It's in the middle of the abandoned entertainment square. Right in the center of—"

"Cosmic fucking Castle?" Gwen nearly shouted. "Holy shit, that's so funny."

"What..." Morgan stared between them, completely lost. "What's Cosmic Castle?"

"An old amusement park," Aaron said, still laughing. "Place has been abandoned since I was a kid."

"People say it's haunted," Gwen added, getting a gleam in her eye. "Kids will dare each other to go sit on the throne."

"Aaron..." Morgan's eyes snapped to his. "...it's *All Hallows' Eve*. If anyone was going to sneak in for a thrill..."

Aaron's mirth vanished instantly. "Armory. Now."

Eerie silence spread over the barren asphalt of the old entertainment square, broken only by four sets of footsteps as Morgan, Aaron, Gwen and Lance approached the rusted gate warning people away from the area with a graffitied metal sign. Not wanting to waste time changing, they looked like a group of children out to collect treats instead of warriors out to combat a threat.

"Why did they close it down?" Morgan mused, clenching a fist to snap the chains barring the way.

Aaron shrugged, pulling the gate open. "No one knows. Some people say they shut down temporarily for renovations, then just never reopened."

"There was a weird string of deaths," Gwen muttered ominously, following Morgan into the square, Lancelot right behind her and Aaron bringing up the rear. "First an employee got crushed by the machinery—"

"Guinevere, I checked the last time we talked about this, that did not happen," Aaron growled.

"Did so!"

"What machinery?" Aaron sassed, wagging his head. "What was their name? Why wasn't it all over the news?"

Morgan raised his brows at Lance, sharing a silent snicker as their partners bickered. Nearby storefronts had been boarded up, closed signs taped over their doors and windows. Empty popcorn bags and plastic wrappings littered the street. Gazing out across the square, he spotted a dark shape ahead, looming over the outline of twisting rails and a Ferris wheel—a rising tower surrounded by small turrets.

"Sad excuse for a castle," Morgan droned, walking ahead. He shot a glance over his shoulder back to Aaron and Gwen, still locked in a hushed argument. "Pipe down, you two. Are there any dispatches en route?"

Aaron rolled his eyes at Gwen with a huff, reaching for his temple. "Doesn't look like it. They're not going to consider this a priority, given its isolation from civilians. Could be hours till they bother."

Giving him a single nod, Morgan broke into a jog. "Let's move."

Once festive and cheerful colors came into sight. Bright blue and red striped signs had faded and chipped away. Neon letters had shattered and turned dark.

Cosmic Castle—Reach for the Stars!

A chill washed over Morgan's skin as he stepped through the arched entrance, followed by a sickening twist in his gut. The rift lay dead ahead, darker than the surrounding night and crackling with menacing energy. While being in the vicinity of a tear in the fabric of reality generally came with raised hairs on the back of one's neck, the dread coursing through Morgan's veins was beyond anything he'd experienced from them thus far.

"Do... Do you guys feel that too?" Gwen rasped, hugging her arms to herself.

Lance placed a hand on her shoulder, nodding darkly. "Everything in me is telling me to run."

"Morgan..." Aaron stepped up behind him, taking his hand. "...what... is this?"

"Do you see anything?" Morgan said quietly, scanning the area. "Anything that would've come out of the rift?"

"Let me check Daphne's scanner," his boyfriend muttered, tapping his comm.

Calliope music screeched to life suddenly. Lights powered on with the sound of breakers being flipped, section by section of the park blaring to life. A carousel nearby began spinning, faster and faster, a whirlwind of four-legged creatures.

"*Reach for the stars!*" a distorted electronic speaker crackled above. "*Reach for the stars! Reach for the—*"

Morgan whipped his arm toward the speaker, sending a bolt of purple light flying, creating a hail of sparks as it collided.

"*Reach... for the...*"

"What... in the seven circles..." Morgan hissed, spinning on the spot.

"Oh-ho-ho, this is so fucking cool," Gwen chuckled despite the way her entire body trembled. "I mean... I hate it. But *cool*."

"This doesn't make any sense," Aaron uttered, shaking his head. "Daph's tech is meant to pick up trace readings of rift energy that clings to whatever came through, but..."

"What, baby?"

"It's... everywhere..." he whispered, meeting Morgan's eyes. "According to this, the whole park came through the rift."

Morgan reached into a small satchel belted to his leg, whipping out his phone. "Daph, you seeing these readings?"

"Morg—are you—" the line crackled with heavy static. "Noth—get out—"

"Daph?" Morgan pulled the phone away, staring at the screen. "Hang on, I think the rift is interfering with the line!" He jogged back toward the entrance, only to come face to face with a solid concrete wall. "What... the fuck?!"

"Where..." Aaron gasped. "How did..."

Morgan snapped his phone shut, shoving it into his pocket. He thrust both hands at the wall, eyes dancing with violet light. The concrete cracked, and he pushed harder, forcing the breaks to spread. Suddenly the wall rippled like water—and the cracks vanished.

"Less cool..." Gwen said, sinking back into Lance. "Much less cool."

With a roar, Morgan lunged forward, his fist burning with light as it collided with the wall. Another ripple shot through the concrete, and Morgan went flying backward.

"Shit!" Aaron shouted, leaping into his path just in time to catch him.

"Fuck you, wall!" Morgan spat.

"What in the hells is happening?" Lance breathed, staring at the wall.

Standing upright and shaking out his hand, Morgan whirled around, glaring. "The amusement park was already here, right? All of this didn't come out of the rift. Something is affecting the entire space somehow."

"What could do that?" Gwen asked, finding her nerve as she strode over to a cotton candy stand. "Ooh! Fairy floss!" She snatched a paper cone from behind the counter, twirling a small pink cloud wrapped in plastic.

"Don't touch anything, Guinevere," Aaron said sharply. "Definitely don't *eat* anything."

"I wasn't going to," she pouted, dropping the sweet onto the ground. The moment it hit the asphalt, it vanished. "Okay, seriously. What the fuck?"

"Okay..." Morgan muttered, pacing toward the carousel. "Okay... we know something from that rift is here, otherwise it wouldn't still be open."

"Babe, I've been fighting shit from the rifts for years," Aaron breathed, shaking his head. "Nothing that can do this kind of crap has ever come through."

"But that doesn't mean it *can't*," Morgan said, waving a hand around. "The rifts are essentially cracks in the fabric of reality, implying damage or a wound. If that damage isn't repaired..."

"It will only get worse," Lance sighed.

"Wounds get infected," Morgan continued. "So far, the things we've seen that come through are seeking either shelter or food. They all have a reason, though."

"They *do* just show up and cause destruction a lot, Morgan," Gwen said.

"They're scared," Morgan said sadly with a shake of his head. "Wherever they come from... it's nothing like Etna. It's loud and different here. Potentially chaotic in comparison."

"So, they act like any frightened animal." Aaron pulled his sword from his belt, giving it a twirl. "Doesn't make putting them down feel great."

Morgan turned back to him with a sympathetic smile. "They're already lost, baby. You can see it in their eyes. Those red flecks of light. The way they break into dust. They're empty, running on nothing but instinct."

"I came through a rift just fine," Lance said with a shrug.

"A puzzle for another day, man," Aaron chuckled. "So... what is this thing after? What does it need?"

"Well, *keeping* us here seems to be a priority," Gwen grumbled, wafting a hand toward the wall. She turned to face the middle of the park, putting her hands on her hips. "If you try to eat us, I promise you that Morgan will give you indigestion!"

"Rude," Morgan whined.

"Is she wrong?" Aaron snickered.

Shooting him a glare, Morgan stomped his foot. "That's it. I'm wearing a cape for the rest of my life."

"No, I take it back!" Aaron groaned.

"Guys..." Lance said loudly, jutting his chin toward the castle.

Morgan's head snapped in the direction he indicated. That sick fear churned in his gut as he glimpsed a silhouetted figure, hardly illuminated by the park lights. Almost human in shape, it stood at least seven feet tall, its limbs stretched beyond any normal proportions with its hands nearly dragging on the ground.

"What the fuck is that?" Aaron whispered, taking a step closer to Morgan.

Without a word, Morgan ran toward the figure, throwing out his hand to summon his sword in a flash of violet. The shape's head turned toward him. Two pinpricks of yellow light blazed in the dark, near blinding. Morgan's arm went to his eyes, shielding them. When he finally dared another glance, the creature had vanished.

"Morgan..." Aaron jogged up behind him, Caliburn at the ready. "Where did it go?"

Morgan whirled back to Gwen. "I need to know everything you know about the rumors surrounding this park, Guinevere. No matter how crazy. Every detail."

The many, many stories involving Cosmic Castle seemed to have no real rhyme or reason, and with the interference in the area, none of them were able to use the city net to clarify. One story mentioned the poor employee of the park dying in a tragic machinery malfunction. One rumor spoke of a young couple that took a ride in the tunnel of love, never to return. And another—Morgan's least favorite—implied that the clowns that had once filled the park feasted on human flesh.

It seemed as if every single attraction came attached with a tale of horror, yet none had ever been confirmed. So, with nothing but a theory after witnessing the creature that didn't quite fit into any of those tales, Morgan led the way through the park, keeping careful watch for any flesh-eating clowns.

"Babe," Aaron asked after him as he stomped ahead, scanning the perimeter, "what are we looking for? Did you recognize that thing?"

"Possibly," Morgan said over his shoulder, eyeing the roller coaster track above. "Testing something. Please hold."

"Testing what?" Aaron groaned, picking up his pace.

"Where might one get killed by machinery?" Morgan mused, pausing in his tracks and thumbing his lower lip.

"No one... ever said where," Gwen panted, clacking along with her dress hitched up in both hands. "They just said... the machinery."

"Which just proves my point," Aaron grumbled. "It *never happened.*"

"Oh, hush." Gwen stuck her tongue out at him. "You know, the skeptic always dies first in the horror movies."

A ghoulish groan echoed across the pavement from a nearby pavilion, unheard by the others as they squabbled.

"Good," Lance groaned, rolling his eyes. "Let something threaten Aaron. Then Morgan can just blow the whole place up and we can return home."

"Did you just make me the bait?!" Aaron gasped indignantly, holding a hand to his chest. "What kind of knight *are* you?"

"Uh... hey..." Morgan muttered, eyeing the start of the roller coaster's track as a bloody hand wrapped around the door to the pavilion.

"The kind that wants to go back to the *party*," Lance said grinning.

"Hey!" Morgan shouted, watching in horror as a mangled figure stumbled out onto the asphalt, dragging its feet and dripping blood. "That our dead employee?"

"Ew..." Gwen sputtered, clapping her hands over her mouth. She took a step away, reaching for the bow strapped to her back. "Ew, ew, *EW!*" she let loose with an arrow, sending it sailing straight for the corpse's head, only to pierce right through as if the creature were made of smoke.

"What?" Aaron croaked, grabbing Morgan's arm to haul him back. "What is it?!"

The corpse shuddered, mangled features twisting in rage as it tore toward them.

"Theory confirmed," Morgan rattled off, taking Aaron's hand and bolting in the other direction. "Run, run, run!"

"I'm wearing *heels!*" Gwen squealed.

"Whose fault is that?!" Aaron shouted back.

Lancelot scooped Gwen up in his arms, causing her to scream as she wrapped her arms around his neck, burying her face in his shoulder. "Can it hurt us?!"

"Don't know," Morgan panted, making a beeline toward the castle at the center of the park. "Not sticking around to find out."

"What did you learn, Morgan?!" Gwen growled after him.

"It's an engregor!"

"A *what?!*"

"Something I read about in one of Merlin's books!" he shouted, hauling Aaron around a corner. "It feeds off of rumors and stories—actually makes them real!"

"How real?!" Aaron breathed, glancing back over his shoulder.

"Well... considering we're very, *very* aware of it's existence right now..." Morgan rasped, trying with all his might not to think of the other stories about the place, "I'd bet it can probably—"

A wild cackle sent chills down Morgan's spine as a knife went spinning through the air right in front of them, lodging itself in a nearby beam wrapped in lights.

"Flesh-eating *clown!*" he screamed, catching a glimpse of striped, baggy clothing and curly red hair before wheeling around in another direction.

"How do we fight them?!" Aaron shouted, ducking another knife as it flew over his head.

"We don't!" Morgan bellowed as another clown materialized in the street dead ahead. He dove into Aaron, knocking him into the bushes to avoid more projectile cutlery.

"Babe..." Aaron rasped beneath him. "What do we do?"

"I'm thinking... I'm thinking..." He racked his brain, trying to ignore the unhinged laughter approaching them from all sides. "It feeds on stories... on psychic energy created when people get scared or even think about—"

Aaron grabbed his face in both hands, crushing their lips together.

Silky smooth lips on his. Sandalwood and citrus clouded his senses. Every shred of fear melted away, replaced in an instant by heat and desire. Aaron. Nothing but Aaron.

"Seriously, guys?" Gwen droned behind them, snapping them out of their short-lived fever.

Morgan pulled away, leaping out of the brush. He whirled around on the spot, searching the street. It was only the four of them.

"You..." Morgan turned back to Aaron where he groaned to his feet, grabbing his hand and pulling him into another bruising kiss. "Fucking *genius!*"

Aaron giggled, giving him an adorable shrug. "You get up in your head all the time. Only one surefire way to stop it."

Gwen belted a laugh, falling back into Lance and shaking her head. "And once again, a kiss saves the day. You two are such a fucking trope."

"Jealous," Morgan said, unable to stop grinning. He blew out a breath, pacing back into the middle of the street. "Okay... so... one of these rumors has to have a resolution."

"Like what?" Lance asked.

"Some kind of... I don't know, happy ending?"

Aaron pursed his lips, looking around. "It's an amusement park, right? Even with all the creepy surrounding the place, there's gotta be some joy in it."

Morgan's eyes drifted around the space. They'd ended up in the central courtyard just outside the castle at the center. Lights flashed and danced on every corner. Music echoed in the distance. He turned to the towers beside them, staring up at the high windows at the top. Spotting another neon sign right in the middle of the center tower, his eyes widened.

"Reach for the stars!"

"Gwen," he breathed. "You said kids would dare each other to get into the castle, right?"

"Uh... yeah," she said quietly, coming up behind him and following his gaze. "They just had to go sit on the throne."

Morgan jerked his head toward the flashing sign at the top of the castle. "Is the throne up there?"

Holding tight to Aaron's hand the entire trek up to the throne room, Morgan managed to keep his thoughts in check. Gwen hummed a song as they climbed cheap wooden steps covered in weathered red carpet, bobbing her head and distracting herself. There was no way of knowing if Morgan's plan would actually work, but it was the only lead they had.

When they reached the top of the steps, Aaron peered through a battered archway before turning back. "All clear."

Morgan let go of Aaron's hand, scanning the musty old room. The whole of the park spread out through a wide window on the opposite wall. That same cheap, red carpet ran down the middle of the floor, leading the way to a massive, poorly constructed throne covered in graffiti.

"Your Majesty." Gwen bowed gracefully, holding out a hand toward the set with a bow in Morgan's direction.

"Why do *I* have to sit?" he grumbled, furrowing his brow. He jabbed a thumb at Aaron. "*He's* the King."

"*You're* the one that conjured the creepy murder clowns and the walking dead just by thinking about them," Aaron said, grinning as he leaned against the side of the throne. "Besides, I've done my time."

Rolling his eyes, Morgan sulked toward the throne. "I don't know what's going to happen. Be ready for anything."

"What if it doesn't work?" Lance asked, gripping his sword at his belt. "Do we have a backup plan?"

"Uh... well..." Morgan cocked his head to the side, lifting his brows. "Next move would be to think *really* hard about the rumors, hope they all become corporeal and hack away."

"Yay..." Gwen groaned.

"Let's... try this first," Aaron nodded to the throne.

Morgan huffed a laugh, then practically threw himself into the rickety chair.

For a moment, nothing happened at all. The music of the park entrance drifted up through the window. Aaron's quiet breaths rustled the hair at the top of his head. Morgan recalled the creature's eyes when it had looked at him, imagining those blinding yellow lights.

Suddenly, a tall shape filled the room in front of him. From the floor right up to the battered wooden planks of the ceiling. Twisted flesh ran over its limbs like the gnarled bark of a tree. Bones were visible beneath, jutting out sharply at its waist and chest. Its bright eyes narrowed on Morgan, searching within the sunken slopes of its skull.

Aaron drew his blade, taking a step toward it when Morgan threw out a hand. "Don't!"

Turning to him in question, Aaron lifted his brows.

"Don't, baby..." Morgan breathed, shaking his head. "It's a creature of thought. Blades won't harm it. I think... I think it has to be reasoned with."

With a nod, Aaron stepped back, sheathing his sword before resting a hand on Morgan's shoulder.

"Hello there," Morgan whispered in awe.

The engregor twisted its head, glancing at each person in the room, then turned back to Morgan. It bowed.

Sorrow blossomed in Morgan's chest. Confusion. Terror. Images of every horrible thing the citizens of Etna had whispered about Cosmic Castle flashed in his mind.

"You poor thing..." Morgan muttered.

"Morgan?" Aaron called softly behind him.

"It... it doesn't know any better." He stood, stepping closer to the creature. "I understand... I woke up here too. I had no idea who I was—where I was. All I could see were the terrible things this world had to offer."

A low moan came from the engregor. It sank to its knees, leaning down to rest its head against Morgan's.

"But I promise you..." he whispered, filling his mind with all the beautiful things he'd found there in Etna. The laughing faces of his friends. The shining city lights as they whirled around him while he and Aaron sped down the endless streets. Vibrant dance beats and moments of revelry in the night. His home. Wrapped up tight in warm, welcoming arms at the end of every day, no matter how trying. "...there is so much more than heartbreak here."

The creature's moan rose in pitch. The light in its eyes burst through the room, pouring out the window and across the park as it sang, ringing out with a beautiful song, returning the gift Morgan had given with a swell of hope.

"You... are so welcome, my friend." Morgan rasped, blinking a tear free as he opened his eyes.

The engregor had gone.

A twisting screech echoed from the park below, followed by a crack like lightning.

Morgan's phone vibrated in his satchel almost immediately after the rift had closed. He whipped it out with a smile, wiping his cheek. "All good, Daph."

"What the hells happened?!" she shouted through the line. "The whole area went dark! I couldn't even ping Aaron or Gwen's comms for a good hour!"

"Long story," Morgan sighed, turning back to Aaron with a bright smile. "But I promise it's a good one."

Last Solstice, Aaron was given a wish…

Still unknown to the boys, their paths had come so close to crossing on that fateful night. Now, Aaron has all that he wished for—and he's making plans to keep it forever.

Wrapping up the tale of the Snow Rose was such a delight. I hope you enjoy it as much as I do.

This short was released on November 29th, 2024

A Very Sapphire Solstice

12.21.204 UI

'Twas the night before Solstice, and all through Fell Manor, holiday cheer overwhelmed with tinsel and candles, even a bright, sparkling banner. Hearth, conjured with magic, sat glowing with embers 'neath digital display of the living room, where sat lone coven member. A king no longer, yet royalty all the same, face buried in a laptop screen—Aaron Jones was his name.

The last two and a half months of Aaron's life had been an absolute whirlwind of joy, passion and peace. Everything he'd been feeling for so many years finally made sense. He was whole, complete in more ways than one.

Briefly tearing his eyes away from an archived news article, he glanced over his shoulder down the hall where the door to Morgan's bedroom—their bedroom—cracked open ever so slightly. Thankfully, their first annual Solstice Eve party at the Majesty had tuckered his boyfriend out to the point of exhaustion, and gentle snores drifted into the hall.

Keeping secrets from Morgan wasn't a skill Aaron had ever honed. He'd never needed to. Never wanted to. Morgan was his confidant, his best friend and his other half. Which made Aaron's necessity to hide his research all the more guarded.

With a click of his finger, the article on his screen flitted away, revealing another page full of text and bearing an image of the most radiant, sparkling stone he'd ever laid eyes on. Gorgeous tones of blue and purple coalesced along shining facets, cut round to perfection—a jewel gone missing nearly three decades past, its whereabouts nothing more than rumor and whispers.

A sanctioned artifact with a tragic tale, the stone had been sought over and again through blood and fire on only the hope that its story bore some semblance of truth. The Dusk Star, said to be capable of reuniting its owner with love lost.

To the world outside the Manor, it might seem as though Aaron and Morgan had only been together for almost three months time, but Aaron had waited long enough.

"What are you doing up at this hour?"

Nearly leaping off the sofa, Aaron slapped the laptop shut with a force he worried might have damaged the device, whipping around to face the hall opposite his bedroom. Taking in dark skin and a tangle of braids, he heaved a breath, clutching his chest. "Hecate's tits, Daph. I'm too young for a heart attack."

Daphne broke into a smirk, giving him a shrug before padding into the kitchen. "I dunno, technically, aren't you like fif—"

"Oh, shut it," he snapped. "My *body* is too young for cardiac problems. What's got you up at—" Aaron tapped at his temple, checking the time on his comm. "Oh, shit. Four in the morning."

With a soft giggle and a shake of her head, Daphne grabbed two teacups from the cupboard. She jabbed a finger at a kettle on the stove, and the contents heated almost instantly, spewing steam out of the spout. "I never went to sleep. Shane just conked out about twenty minutes ago, but I can't get out of my head."

"You wanna talk about it?" Aaron offered, leaning back on the sofa. "I'm wide awake now, thank you very much."

"Nah," Daphne breathed, pouring the tea before rounding the counter to sit beside Aaron. She passed him one of the steaming mugs with a smile. "They're all good thoughts. A bit scary, but good. I think."

Aaron hummed, nodding. He took a sip of his tea, soothing chamomile hitting his tastebuds. "I hear that."

Daphne's grin stretched. "So... the Dusk Star, huh? Planning countermeasures in case something goes sideways in the future?"

Nearly choking on his tea with a laugh, Aaron shook his head. He set the cup down on the coffee table, chewing his lip for a moment. "Uh... no. I mean, maybe? I guess? But not because of its legend. I can't find any legitimate proof that the thing is actually magical. It's nothing but stories."

"I'm a little familiar with it," Daphne said, eyes flitting over Aaron's shoulder toward the hall where Morgan's snores still wafted quietly into the living room. "Your boyfriend would know more, though. He lives on legends like that."

Aaron chuckled, beaming at the mention of his witch. "Yeah, I have no doubt about that, but..."

"But?" Daphne pressed, still grinning from ear to ear. When Aaron shot her a mild glare, she continued, "Aaron Jones, hiding away in the dead of night to keep his fascination with a pretty rock secret from his soulmate? A rock that just happens to share shades of blue and violet? Whatever could he be up to?"

"Maybe I just want to get him a present his money can't buy?" Aaron pouted, crossing his arms over his chest.

"A present that says 'be mine forever'?"

Aaron snorted at the thought. "I think that ship has sailed, made port, been deconstructed and repurposed into a house, Daph. The future might be uncertain, but I know Morgan is there until the day I die. Again."

"Bleak..." Daphne lifted her brows over her teacup, taking a drink. "How does that even work? I've never met another common-witch couple that's been bound. If you share his magic, do you share his lifespan?"

With a shrug, Aaron grabbed his teacup, taking a deep swig. "Morgan says at least a couple hundred years, minimum. Probably longer, given how strong his magic is."

"And then he'll just find a way to bring you back again, no doubt," Daphne chuckled. "You know... if there's anywhere to bring you back to by then."

Aaron gave her a wry laugh. "We don't need forever, Daph. Just *our* forever."

"Ugh, stop," she groaned, setting her empty teacup on the table. "Not gonna be able to sleep if your shared cuteness makes me sick to my stomach."

"Your ninja-like appearance still has my pulse racing, so turnabout is fair play."

Daphne smiled, pulling her legs up to her chest with both arms wrapped around her knees. "You're really not gonna tell me—"

"Nope," Aaron said, grinning as he stood. He gulped down the rest of his tea, suddenly needing nothing more than to wrap his arms around his boyfriend.

"Aww... come on, Aar-bear..." Daphne whined.

Aaron chuckled at the nickname she'd only recently begun using, usually when she wanted something. He shook his head at her as she continued to pout from the sofa, glaring while he set his cup in the sink and turned toward the bedroom.

"I can keep a secret!" she pressed as he walked away.

"No one in this house can keep a secret," Aaron chuckled, "and that's saying something given whose house it is."

"Ugh, fine," Daphne growled. "Happy Solstice, buttmunch!"

"Happy Solstice, Daph," Aaron said quietly as he pushed the bedroom door open. He smiled wide at the sight of the man he intended to spend his forever with, passed out and drooling on his pillow. Carefully, he crawled into bed, tucking one arm beneath Morgan's neck and wrapping the other around his waist to pull him tight to his chest. "Happy Solstice, beautiful."

***

Morgan was roused from the deepest of sleeps, warm and tingly from head to toe. His face was buried in a mass of muscle, pressed between Aaron's pecs. Their legs were tangled together beneath the sheets, Morgan's body held in place against his boyfriend's in the most possessive of cuddles.

Right where he belonged.

As his conscious thoughts took over, he noticed a slight discomfort in his briefs, the fabric stretched taut by morning wood. Morgan shifted his hips forward gently, curious if his cock was the only one up and ready to start the day. He smiled, licking his lips as his hardened length met Aaron's.

A gentle chuckle rustled his hair. "Good morning to you too."

Morgan slipped his hands beneath the hem of Aaron's t-shirt, running his fingertips over the peaks and valleys of his stomach as he lifted the fabric. "Happy Solstice, baby," he whispered, placing his lips over a nipple to suck it between his teeth.

"Mmpf..." Aaron groaned, moving a hand down to Morgan's ass with a squeeze. "Best Solstice ever."

Snickering, Morgan trailed over Aaron's abs, kissing each one as he shimmied down, down, down until he was level with the bulge in his pajama pants. He ran his lips over the outline of Aaron's cock, wetting the fabric, breathing deep with his nose in his sack. Getting high on his scent and making his own dick swell impossibly harder.

Aaron gripped the back of his head, pushing his face into his crotch with a groan. "You want that, sweetheart?"

"Mhmm..." Morgan grunted against him.

Curling his fingers in Morgan's hair, Aaron pulled him away before shoving his pants down. Morgan licked his lips as his cock came free, opening wide. Aaron pushed his dick down, angling it toward his face, offering.

Morgan wrapped his lips around the head, humming with delight at the taste of him, dancing around the skin therewith the tip of his tongue.

"Oh, that feels so good, Morgan..." Aaron shuddered, tightening his hold on Morgan's hair. "...so fucking good."

Palming Aaron's balls with one hand, Morgan sucked him down to the back of his throat, working his length with tongue and lips as he went. He gave Aaron's hip a gentle shove, urging him onto his back, following to kneel between his legs.

Aaron placed his other hand over the one in Morgan's hair, rolling his hips in time with his pulls.

"Mmf..." Morgan choked through his mouthful as Aaron fucked his face, bracing himself with both hands around thick, muscled thighs. He relaxed his throat, letting Aaron thrust deeper, breathing in the fine hairs at his waist. Nothing brought him more of a thrill than when his king took control—when he could let his walls down, submitting to the only person deserving of his deference.

"Fuck, sweetheart..." Aaron growled, bright blue eyes locked on Morgan's as he held him in place. "You're so fucking beautiful with my cock down your throat. I'm going to come just from watching you."

"*Come for me,*" Morgan begged, speaking directly into his mind. "*I want it, baby. I need it.*"

Aaron's stomach contracted at the plea. His thighs tightened, trembling beneath Morgan's grip. "I'm... so close..." His jaw fell with panting breaths, brows furrowed above wide eyes, yearning desperately for his witch to take him over the edge. "Stroke yourself for me, Morgan. Come with me."

Releasing one of Aaron's thighs, Morgan reached into his briefs, already damp with his arousal. His fingers curled around his own cock, precome slicking his skin as he stroked urgently.

"That's it, sweetheart..." Aaron groaned, his eyes rolling back in his head. "...that's my boy."

Morgan grunted around Aaron's cock, already coming undone. Aaron's scent in his nose. His taste in his mouth. His praise echoing in his head. Electricity ripped down his spine. Aaron's fingers coiled tighter in his hair, shoving his face into his waist.

"*Arthur...*" Morgan sang into his head, "*...Arthur.*"

Aaron whimpered somewhere above him. He arched his back, trembling from head to toe as his cock exploded in Morgan's mouth. Hot bursts of come shot down his throat, one after another.

The taste sent him soaring as he gulped down every drop, his own release tearing through him, drenching his hand, the sheets between his knees and the back of Aaron's leg. He buried his face in Aaron's waist, his cock still pulsing against Morgan's tongue as their shared highs slowly subsided.

Aaron let out a blissful sigh, dropping his head back into the pillows. He swiped his hand along the back of his leg where Morgan had painted it with come, and pressed his fingers between his lips with a smile.

Morgan pulled away from his softening cock, giving the head one last lick for good measure before climbing over Aaron to fall onto his chest. "Hi."

Aaron chuckled, wrapping him up in his arms. "Hey there, beautiful."

"I love wake-up sex with you." Morgan muttered against his skin.

"You love any sex with me."

"Fair point."

Kissing the top of his head, Aaron brushed his hair back. "The others are probably waiting on us."

"For what?" Morgan groaned, craning his neck to meet his eyes.

"It's Solstice, silly," Aaron said with an airy laugh. "We have *presents* to open."

Giving a disinterested shrug, Morgan dropped his cheek back to Aaron's chest. "I got my present. I'm good."

Aaron belted a laugh, rolling them over to their sides. Morgan whined, locking his arms tight around Aaron's back. "*Nooooo... this* is my Solstice. Right here."

"Come on," Aaron said, reaching down to tug Morgan's briefs free of his ankle, flinging them across the room. He latched both hands around the back of his thighs, lifting him from the bed to carry him to the bathroom. "Shower, presents, holiday cheer, then you can have another present before bed."

"*Fiiiine.*"

Aaron sat in the large red armchair beside the fireplace Morgan had conjured from thin air beneath the digital display of the living room. A towering Solstice tree laden with sparkling ornaments in violet and blue—that the two of them may have decorated all by themselves—stood proudly between the hearth and the door to the balcony, a halfway picked through heap of presents beneath.

Morgan paced the living room in his black silk pajamas and a dark blue hoodie of Aaron's, passing out gifts between their not so little family. Daphne was hugging a large, leather-bound tome to her chest, nearly in tears as he turned away with a bright smile.

"Morgan..." she breathed, tracing the design burned into the leather with her fingertips, "...it's *beautiful*. Thank you."

"You're very welcome, love," Morgan called back to her sweetly as he plucked a large envelope from beneath the tree. "I know you prefer cataloguing your spells digitally, but it's a right of passage for a teacher to give an apprentice their own grimoire. Totally up to you how you use it."

"I love it," Daphne choked, clutching the book tighter.

Aaron hid his face to wipe away an escaped tear the exchange had caused, bracing himself as Morgan handed the envelope to Gwen, where she sat on a loveseat cuddled up with Lancelot.

"What's this?" She shot Morgan a suspicious look, then glanced at Aaron.

"A pony," Morgan said flatly, gliding back to Aaron to swing his legs over the arm of the chair and drop into his lap. He caught Aaron's eye, sucking his lip between his teeth with a grin.

"*She's going to scream,*" Aaron whispered into his head.

"*Good scream or mad scream?*" Morgan asked.

"*Yes.*"

"This title deed for the property of..." Gwen's jaw fell. She leapt to her feet, eyes bulging out of her skull. "WHAT?!"

"Told you," Aaron droned.

"Are you serious?!" Gwen shouted, her eyes welling over with tears.

"What is it?" Lance stood, concern etched all over his face as he placed both hands on her shoulders.

Gwen clapped a hand over her mouth with a stifled sob. "It's a land deed... a new salon... oh my gods, it's on *Beat Street!*"

Morgan chuckled happily, nestling his head beneath Aaron's chin.

"You guys..." Gwen choked, "...this is... holy hells, this is so wonderful, but..." She shook her head, collecting herself. "I can't accept this. This is too much."

"Too late," Morgan and Aaron said in unison.

"Seriously, do you have any idea how many stylists want a spot like this?"

"All of them?" Aaron offered with a shrug.

"All of them," Gwen nodded. "I'm *barely* known in this city, I can't claim a spot like this!"

"Well, to be fair, it's for both you and Dani," Morgan said. "And technically, the coven owns the property."

"So... I'd just be renting a chair?" Gwen raised her brows, suddenly breathing easier.

"If that makes you feel better," Morgan snickered. "You try to give me any rent and you'll find it hacked right back into your account, though."

Gwen laughed, shaking her head with tears in her eyes as she leaned back into Lancelot. "I hate you both."

"You're welcome." Morgan beamed at her, wrapping an arm around Aaron's neck.

Aaron kissed the top of his head, squeezing him tight. Shane sat beside Daphne, watching her thumb through the blank pages of her new grimoire, the brand-new rune etching tools they'd gotten him in his lap. Frey was rifling through a satchel full of some of the most exotic plant seeds Morgan had been able to get his hands on. Percival was holding up items from a pile of new clothes to his chest, Gawain at his side, admiring a handsome dagger.

"Did the two of you already exchange gifts?" Lance asked as he ushered Gwen back to their seat.

"As soon as we woke up," Morgan chuckled, biting his lip.

"Gross," Daphne sighed, rolling her eyes.

"Babe," Aaron chided, poking his side. In truth, they'd decided not to get anything for one another, simply because neither of them could think of any material items that would mean more to them than their first holiday back together.

"Well..." Morgan met Aaron's eyes with a wary look. "I... did actually get you something. It's sort of for both of us, though." He turned to Frey where they sat on the carpet beneath the coffee table.

The fairy immediately leapt to their feet with a glowing smile, darting down the hall. "I got it!"

"Sweetheart..." Aaron searched his face questioningly.

"Don't be mad at me." Morgan pouted, jutting out his bottom lip. "It's just a silly little thing."

"*You* do not give silly gifts, Morgan le Fay," Aaron growled with a smirk. "You only give thoughtful, meaningful and downright outrageous presents, otherwise it's not worth your time."

"Exhibit A." Daphne held up her grimoire.

"And B." Gwen chuckled, flapping the envelope that held the deed to the salon in front of her.

Frey's footsteps thundered down the hall as they came back into the room, holding a small, white pot in their palms. Aaron's mouth fell open as his eyes trailed up a long, thorned stem, landing on powder blue, heart-shaped petals. "Morgan... is that..."

"Do you remember the first time I gave you one?" Morgan asked softly, taking the pot from Frey with a smile and setting it in his lap.

Aaron brushed the petals tenderly with his fingertips. "They were so rare... even back then. I'd never seen one until you took me to that clearing in the woods."

Morgan hummed a teary-eyed laugh. "I... never told you, but... I made a silent wish that Solstice. I was sitting right next to you in the woods, just staring at that single, stubborn rose in the snow, and... I couldn't help myself."

"What did you wish?" Aaron breathed, tearing his eyes from the flower to meet Morgan's love-drunk stare.

"For you to follow your heart," Morgan uttered, barely audible. "Whatever that meant."

Aaron sucked in a sharp breath, tears prickling along his lashes. "That... that was Solstice right before—"

"Before you kissed me," Morgan rasped, nodding.

"Oh, *fy cariad*," Aaron choked, grabbing his face in both hands to kiss him deeply, chuckling against his lips. Suddenly he pulled away, searching Morgan's eyes. Another memory of the flower breaking through. "Oh my gods..."

"What is it?" Morgan whispered, tracing Aaron's jaw with his fingertips.

"Last year..." He looked across the room, catching Gwen's eyes, "...at the Spire! Someone left me a drink with a Snow Rose in it!"

"Holy shit, they did!" Gwen said, her brows jumping. "Those weren't real, though, were they? Benny just colored some cheap carnations or something."

"That one was real..." Morgan breathed, eyes wide and locked on Aaron's face. "I know... I... was the one who turned it into the genuine article."

Aaron jerked back in his chair, searching Morgan's eyes. "Y-You left it? You saw me there?"

With a gentle shake of his head, Morgan let out an airy chuckle. "I had no idea. I was there for a job, and Benny tried taunting me into making a wish! I was just showing off and told him to give it to someone who deserved it."

Sputtering a laugh, Aaron leaned down, resting his forehead against Morgan's. "Wow... I can't believe it. My wish came true and everything."

"What did you wish for?" Morgan asked, his breath rolling over Aaron's lips.

"This," Aaron sighed, full of joyous disbelief. "You."

After a hearty breakfast—with pancakes as the central focus, of course—full of laughter and cheer, surrounded by the ones they loved most, Aaron snuck off to the balcony holding a cup of hot cider, claiming he just needed to cool off. A light dusting of snow covered the metal banister. Carols could be heard from the streets below.

Aaron stared out to the skyline, buzzing with glee. Whether or not the legends of the Snow Rose had anything to do with where his life had taken him, he couldn't say nor care. At last, his Solstice celebrations were full of happiness again.

And he was never letting it go.

"Hey, champ," Daphne's voice came from behind him with the slide of the glass door. "Want some company? It's warm as the hells in there."

"Sure, Daph," he chuckled.

She moved up to his side, resting her elbows on the railing and knocking his shoulder with her own. "You alright there, Your Majesty?"

Aaron belted a laugh. "Alright? I'm on cloud nine."

"Yeah, I can tell," she snickered, shaking her head. "Hey, I wanted to thank you, by the way."

"For the book?" Aaron raised a brow. "I helped pick it out, but that was all Morgan's idea. Said you'd waited long enough for your own grimoire."

"No, not for the book." Daphne shook her head with a smile. "For... I don't know, being here? In our lives, I mean. I've... I've never experienced a celebration like this before, and I can't help but feel like it's all because of you."

"What do you mean?" Aaron gave her a sideways glance with a sad smile.

"Don't get me wrong, Morgan loves Solstice," Daphne said. "We'd always exchange a small gift and have a nice meal. Spend the day reading or something cozy, but..." She hummed a laugh. "...you gave him something, Aaron. I know it was something he had once, long ago, but he was lost without you. This kind of happiness... the way the Manor is just so full of love today, I..."

Aaron shot her a glowing smile. "I get it, Daph. It's not just me, though. It's him. It's all of you. Our little family. It's what we do. Why we fight."

"Yeah," Daphne nodded, delight on her face. She met his eyes, suddenly serious. "I want this forever, you know?"

"Me too, Daph."

"I mean it, Jones," she said sharply, lifting her brows almost accusingly. "If you want help tracking that stone down, I might have a connection that can get us a lead."

Aaron's head jerked up. "Really?"

"Mhm..." Daphne nodded, grinning wickedly. "*If* you can convince me that it's important enough."

Biting his lip to hide his smile, Aaron shook his head, sagging against the banister defeatedly. "You can't tell a soul. Not until I'm ready."

"Tell them what?" Daphne leaned forward, practically shaking with excitement.

"It stays between you and me for as long as possible, but when I do this, I'm going to need all hands on deck."

"When you do *what?*"

"Something I should have done a very, *very* long time ago." Aaron's heart fluttered in his chest. His lips curled into the biggest smile he'd ever mustered as he met Daphne's giddy face. "I'm going to ask Morgan to marry me."

Aaron does not excel at being sneaky.

At least he's got enough charm to woo his way out of a tight spot, and knows how to handle his guy when Morgan's suspicions are roused.

The first exclusive to this collection and so much fun to write, here is Aaron's very first heist…

THE SEARCH FOR—

The Dusk Star

03.14.204 UI

The smell of must and mildew punched Aaron in the face as he dropped into a low crouch on matted green carpet. The dusty, single-paned window he'd slipped through clattered softly as it closed above, plunging the room into darkness. He froze on the spot, listening carefully for any sound of movement. After several minutes of nothing but ringing silence, he reached for his temple. "Think I'm all clear."

"Hit your temp scanner," Daphne said hurriedly in his ear, "just to be sure."

Aaron rolled his eyes, fiddling with the new comm interface she'd been testing for the past few weeks. "It's frickin' City Hall, Daph. Are we being cautious, or am I prototyping?" Blobs of purple, blue and green replaced his vision. He held his own hand up to his face, now a mix of yellow, orange and red.

"Yes," she snapped. "You really want the surprise blown by a five o'clock news report?"

An outside connection with another cipher, a visit to his former precinct building—glamoured to look like another officer of course—months of scouring decades old city files, and several visits to the Etna City Historical Museum, and there Aaron was, hot on the trail of the stone he was going to propose with. Maybe not *hot* on the trail. Lukewarm. Hopefully.

With a sigh, he stood, switching off the heat scan. "Morgan would certainly get a kick out of it."

Daphne chuckled. "He'd never let you live it down."

"Definitely not," Aaron snickered, moving through a dark office space, dodging filing cabinets and shoddy desks. "Man, this place hasn't changed. This furniture is older than me."

"*Aaron* you, or—"

"Ha ha," he droned, pushing open a wooden door that led to the hallway connecting the different branches of the offices. "I think the Ministry of Education was..." Humming, he glanced back and forth down the hall.

"Should be to your right."

"Are we sure the Preservation Board is even part of the Education branch still?" Aaron breathed, slinking toward the door on his right with one gloved hand on the wall to guide him. "They've been getting downsized every year for the last decade."

"We'd better hope," Daphne said. "Otherwise, there's no telling where these files are hiding. Still can't believe they're not on the net. Lucky that Jazz found us the indexes to the hard copies."

"Is it really that surprising?" Aaron muttered, pushing into another musty office. Tugging his sleeve to his elbow, he tapped a rune, summoning a glowing blue orb of light to search the wall of filing cabinets ahead. "We're after documents detailing unlawful possession of a sanctioned artifact. The museum had no business holding onto the stone. They knew that."

Daphne let out a wry laugh. "You ever read up on the British Museum?"

"Extensively," Aaron breathed, tapping another rune before jabbing a finger against the locked cabinet in front of him. The lock clicked, and he pulled the drawer open. "After rifling through records of their lost collection of Arthurian art, that is."

"Little egotistic, champ," Daphne snickered.

"Hey," Aaron growled, rifling through the files, "I didn't know who I was. It was—"

"Oh, shit! Aaron, get down!" Daphne hissed.

"What?" he sputtered, diving behind a desk just as the room's overhead lights flickered on.

"Is someone here?"

Aaron swallowed, forcing his breaths to slow, holding as still as humanly possible.

"I don't know how they skirted around the cameras," Daphne rattled off in a harsh whisper. "Go invisible or something. Get out of there!"

Clenching his teeth, Aaron shook his head, knowing he had no way of responding without alerting the owner of the muffled footsteps that were slowly approaching. He couldn't cloak himself like Morgan could. Though, in that moment, he was baffled as to why the two of them hadn't thought up a rune combination for such a spell yet.

"I'm unarmed," the voice said shakingly. "I might even be able to help you. Just... please, don't hurt me."

Guilt tugged at Aaron's heartstrings. Beyond the panic in their plea, something seemed familiar about the voice. With a sigh, Aaron tapped a *shield* rune just to be safe, grunting to his feet.

"Off–Officer Jones?" A frail, slender woman who was mostly frizzy red hair blinked at him in disbelief behind thick round frames.

Aaron eyed her for a moment, trying to place her freckled face. His brows shot up as he recalled her sitting behind the large reception desk in the lobby, greeting him whenever he'd had official business there. "Anita, was it?"

The woman blushed profusely. "You remember my name?"

"Of course," Aaron said nonchalantly with a shrug and a lopsided grin, tapping his arm to drop his shield. "You saved my butt the first week on the job. How could I forget?"

Just days after graduating from the academy, Chief Bowen had tasked Aaron with sitting in on a meeting with the Ministry of Defense to take notes. He'd been running late after an awful morning, only to arrive at City Hall to find the door to the meeting room locked. Anita had managed to sneak him in through a side door, distracting the occupants of the room with coffee and donuts and leaving them none the wiser. They'd shared friendly smiles every time Aaron had business there since.

Anita peeled a laugh, clapping a hand over her mouth. "Well... maybe I can come to your rescue again. One last time at least."

"What do you mean?" Aaron's brow furrowed.

"I'm here late... trying to finish some paperwork for one of the shelters, but... it's my last day. They sacked me." Anita shrugged, staring down at the floor. "Half the staff too. Said we failed our quality standards, but we all know they're planning a massive turnover. Probably just an excuse."

"What?" Aaron nearly shouted. "Why?"

"Uh..." She eyed the open door to the hall, then stepped closer to Aaron, speaking in a harsh whisper, "We think... they're cutting deals with Esotech. Getting their people into government positions."

Aaron's fingers flew to his comm. "You hearing this, Daph?"

"I'm all over it," she responded instantly, keys clacking away in the background. "Doubt I'll find anything solid until we get our hands on that code we need to break their encryption, though. Esotech will have this on lock down."

"Right," Aaron uttered with a nod. "And I'm no Officer anymore, Anita."

"Oh, right!" she squeaked, shaking her head. "I knew that. Old habits. Anyway, I'm guessing you're here on a job for your boyfriend?"

"Uh... well..."

"It's okay," Anita giggled. "I'm not going to say shit to these bastards. What do you need?"

Aaron cocked his head with a grin. "You sure you want to throw your lot in with mercs? That's a big leap from a government position."

"Says the ex-cop," Daphne chuckled in his ear.

"I don't care," Anita said, smiling from ear to ear. "I don't know if I'll be able to make rent this month because of these jerks. Anything to stick it to them right now. I'm your girl."

Aaron belted a laugh, jutting his head toward the open filing cabinet. "Looking for dirt on the Dusk Star. You know it?"

"Oh!" she squealed, smiling impossibly wider. "I wondered when witches would come sniffing around for that thing! Are you trying to reclaim it for the OC?" Waving for him to follow, Anita led the way to another door in the corner of the room.-

"In... a sense..."

"Okay, keep your secrets, Mister Mercenary," Anita scoffed, punching a code into the keypad beside the door. The locked flashed red. "Seriously?! I haven't even punched out for the day, and they've canceled my access codes?"

"Let me." Aaron sidled up to the keypad, tapping his comm to pull up the slicing tool Daphne had installed. Breaking mechanical locks with runes was one thing, but the only witch Aaron knew who could hack basic digital locks with magic was his boyfriend. The lock flashed green.

"Okay, that's freaking cool," Anita whispered, pushing open the door to a small, cluttered room stacked full of boxes. "So, from what I know, the ECPD considered this cold case, didn't they?"

"Literally two days after the stone went missing, yeah," Aaron growled, leaning back against the wall as Anita perused the boxes. "Even with the deaths involved."

"Deaths?" Anita turned back to him, eyes bulging. "For a material object, I could understand, but with loss of life?"

Aaron nodded darkly. "The only recognizable bodies were members of a gang that went by *The Harlequins*. They disbanded right after the shootout. ECPD didn't care about losing gang members."

Anita perked up as she read a dusty label, wrenching a ragged box free of the stack it was buried under. "This—should be everything we have related to the stone. There's some old camera footage in there too." She held the box out to Aaron. "What are you hoping to find?"

"Records from the museum," Aaron said, setting the box down on another stack to rifle through the contents. "One of the bodies found at the scene was relocated. Everything related to the victim was marked confidential, but when my cipher cracked the files..." Aaron wagged his brows once, pursing his lips. "...completely empty."

"Not one of the Harlequins, then," Anita said with an interested tone.

"Doubtful, the city wouldn't bother hiding that," Aaron muttered, scanning page after page of faded print. "The entire museum staff was let go the day after the stone went missing."

"So, you want access records from the staff entrance to the building," Anita deduced.

Aaron clicked his tongue against his teeth, shooting her a wink. "Maybe you should look into a private investigator's license after this."

Anita chuckled. "Nah. Gods help me, I think I want to do something to help people in this stupid city, but I'm kind of over anything with paperwork."

"You get that, Daph?" Aaron asked calmly, scanning another document as he tapped his comm to put it on speaker.

"I've got three different interviews lined up for her with our affiliates," Daphne said. "All with a personal recommendation from Morgan."

"Wh... What?" Anita's jaw dropped, eyes welling over with tears.

Aaron shrugged, grinning. "Esotech aren't the only ones with their claws in this city. Daph will shoot you the details if you're interested. Totally up to you though."

Anita nearly toppled him over with a bruising hug, then quickly pulled away before he could return it, wiping her eyes. "Thank... thank you. Your coven really is just as wonderful as some people say."

"We're trying." Smiling wide, Aaron shook his head. "And you're helping me out here. It's only fair."

"I brought you to a door that I couldn't even open," Anita chuckled, removing her glasses to dry her cheeks. "Not really a fair trade."

"Eh, you saved my job way back when, remember?" Aaron snickered, flipping to a page that bore nothing but a list of names and times. Near the bottom of the sheet, the form stopped abruptly as if it had been cut off. "Daph, you seeing this?"

"Paydirt," Daphne confirmed. "Cross referencing it with their staffing logs and camera feeds. That stone is as good as ours."

"We're never going to find this thing." The next morning,

Aaron hovered over Daphne's shoulder where she sat in her office, reviewing the tapes Anita had given them. Every staff member had been accounted for, and none of them were well off enough to have fenced the jewel themselves. No missing persons reports. No police calls or even grievances over being fired suddenly. The entire operation seemed to have gone wholly unnoticed by the general public. "Who were they hiding?" he grumbled, running a hand through his hair. "Who could have been important enough to make their name and body just disappear?"

"It had to be a set-up," Daphne sighed, shaking her head as she scoured old camera footage for the twentieth time. "Someone organized this, roped our unsuspecting thief into their scheme, and tipped off the Harlequins to cut out the middleman."

"Sure, but no one else was on the property that day." Aaron waved a hand at the screens. "No signs of a break-in. All former staff are accounted for."

"Maybe one of the staff passed it off on their way home?" Daphne mused, exasperated.

"Unless one of them is living it large without ever spending a single credit, it doesn't add up." Aaron turned away to pace the office, thinking out loud. "They would've either organized it or just been another lackey. Why cut out one middleman and not the other?"

"Maybe it was never about money?" Daphne suggested, pausing the feed on an image of the museum's janitor just before he went off-screen. "Maybe they wanted to use the stone."

Aaron's stomach plummeted at the thought. If somehow the thief had done what no one else seemed capable of and used the Dusk Star's magic to reunite with a lost love, there wouldn't be any sort of paper trail to follow. "You checked—"

"Marriages and engagement announcements. Even relationship updates on social media, where I could find it." Daphne sank back in her chair, studying the image of the janitor. "What is this guy looking at? This camera feed is the main hall, and he's looking over his shoulder toward the lobby, but… it's just the wall."

Aaron paused to assess the feed. The rest of the museum seemed empty, the timestamp reading after closing time. A short balding man held a mop, eyes wide and staring off into a dark corner of the lobby. His mouth parted ever so slightly, either about to gasp or say something. "Play the video, just a few seconds ahead."

Daphne hit play, and the man's lips moved, muttering something before turning away and disappearing into the break room.

"You know," Morgan's voice came from behind, making Aaron's heart shoot into his throat, "if you pull up the blueprints, you'll find there's an old storage closet there with an access tunnel that runs beneath the building."

Daphne slapped the keyboard, minimizing the cameras. Aaron spun on the spot, leaning over to block his boyfriend's view of their project. "Hey, babe!"

Morgan's eyes narrowed. "Secrets don't make friends."

"No secrets," Daphne said, slightly off key with a smile. "Just a little case for Aaron's friend, Anita."

Giving Aaron an assessing scan, he pursed his lips. "You have a friend that robs museums? I like her already."

"Not robbing," Aaron chuckled, moving close to grab Morgan's t-shirt and pull him to his lips. "City Hall sacked her today, and she's looking to get revenge with an old case they covered up."

Aaron berated himself instantly as Morgan's eyes lit up. "Oooh! I wanna help!"

"You *did* help," Aaron said softly, booping his nose with his fingertip. "That access tunnel might be the break we needed."

"Yay me." Morgan gave him a goofy grin, leaning forward to steal another kiss. "Do we get to punch anyone? I need to punch someone."

"We've got this, babe," Aaron laughed airily, shaking his head. "Is everything okay?"

Morgan's brows shot up. "Yeah. Why?"

"You...said you need to punch someone."

"Yeah, it's been like..." Pausing to think, Morgan's eyes shifted back and forth in mental calculation. "...*months* since I've hit someone that needs it. I'm going soft, and it's all your fault, Pendragon." He stabbed Aaron between his pecs with his fingertip. "Let me help."

"We're not going to punch anyone, sweetheart," Aaron snickered, lacing their fingers together. "We're trying to identify a murder victim. Might have to go talk to possible witnesses."

"Potentially emotional moments with strangers?"

"Yes."

"Bye," Morgan droned, rolling his eyes and swaggering away. He paused in the doorway, looking over his shoulder. "Oh, is it the old curator? Did they find him?"

Aaron crossed his arms over his chest, cocking his head. "The old curator?"

"I think his name was..." Morgan's brow furrowed. "Brandt? Brandon? I dunno, something with a B."

"How are you so damn familiar with the museum?" Daphne shook her head with a puzzled look. "We've never run a job there."

"*You've* never run a job there. I get bored easily," Morgan said with a shrug and a wink. "My contact, Dottie, used to work there. She told me about the tunnel so I could sneak in and get an old vase for her. Anyway, she said the guy just vanished right before they replaced the entire staff. Never saw him again."

Aaron laughed through his nose, shaking his head.

"I helped again, didn't I?" Morgan said, dripping with smugness.

"Go away, you brat," Aaron chuckled, rolling his eyes.

"Love you!" Morgan giggled as he disappeared around the corner.

Deep in the South District slums, Aaron and Daphne stood on a shallow stone staircase outside a battered steel door. Aaron gave the button beside the keypad a push, bouncing on the balls of his feet. "You sure this is the place?"

"It's her last known address," Daphne shrugged, dragging her fingertip along her temple. "Not a lot of financial activity on record, but enough to know she's still breathing. And the only name on the list I can see being shortened to 'Dottie.'"

Aaron gave it another moment before pressing the call button again. "Can you tell if anyone is inside? Do that life sense thing Morgan does?"

Daphne's eyes flitted over the front of the building, flashing gold. "Hmmm... I think she's in there. Doesn't seem to be moving, though. Might have a bit of a rat problem too."

Aaron whipped around on the ledge. "You think we were followed?"

"No, actual rats," Daphne chuckled, nodding toward the door. "Smaller life forces around."

"Oh," Aaron's shoulders dropped with a quick exhale. "Thought maybe Morgan trailed us or something."

"With the threat of genuine human connection?" She snickered, shaking her head. "Never."

"Hey, he's not *that* callous," Aaron growled, jabbing the call button one more time. "At least not when it matters. I think I just got it through to him that this was something I wanted to handle alone."

"Aar-bear, you know your boyfriend doesn't just let things go," Daphne droned, smiling. "He knows damn well you're up to something now, but as it's *you* hiding something, he's going to play your game."

With a grumble in his throat, he pursed his lips. She was right on the money. Morgan now knew there was something to know, and was affording Aaron the grace of not pushing simply because he was the one keeping the secret. As long as he didn't know of the connection between this former curator and the Dusk Star—and as the jewel was a sanctioned artifact with a magical history, there was indeed a chance he knew it well—it was fine.

Sighing softly, Aaron moved closer to the door. "It's fine. End of the day, all that matters is making my intentions known. If Morgan sees it coming, then so be it."

"Making your intentions known," Daphne said, laughing. "All those mixed signals of yours—constant heart-shaped eyes, nonstop sex, and the whole coming back from the dead to be together thing. Yeah, he must be so confused."

"Oh, shut up," Aaron said, grinning as he pounded on the front door. "Miss Dillons? My name is Aaron Jones. You hired my boyfriend, Morgan, for a job a while back and I was just hoping to talk."

A faint rustling came from inside the building, followed by hurried footsteps. The door rattled, cracking open just a sliver to reveal a wrinkled face with a mop of gray hair. "Oh. Hello, there." The door opened wider as the woman broke into a bright smile. "My, you are a handsome one, aren't you? Even the news broadcasts don't do you justice."

"Uh... thank you," Aaron chuckled uncomfortably, clutching the back of his head. "I'm so sorry to disturb you, Miss Dillons, but—"

"Oh, not at all, dear," Dorothy chimed, waving them inside. "Pardon the way I ignored the bell. I'm so used to solicitors spouting their anti-witch propaganda in these parts, I tend not to hear it anymore." She led the way through a cluttered mess of a hallway that smelled of old takeout. "Any friend of Morgan's is a friend of mine. He's such a sweet young man."

"Do you keep in touch with him?" Aaron asked, taking a seat at a small dining room table littered with newspapers and magazines.

"Not as much as I'd like these days," she chortled, moving a box out of another chair for Daphne. "But he's a busy boy, isn't he? And who can blame him for not coming around when he's got a strapping fellow like you at home?"

"We are indeed getting rather busy," Aaron sighed, then immediately turned beet red. "With work. And acquiring the orphanage, and running the club, I mean... not..." He hid his face in his hands. "I've been trained in public speaking *twice*. What is wrong with me?"

Daphne and Dottie shared a hearty laugh at his expense as they introduced themselves. "So, you're the brains of the operation, then, are you dear?" Dottie asked, placing a hand over Daphne's on the table. "We love a woman at the helm. Keeps these silly boys in check, doesn't it?"

"Not as often as you'd think." Daphne shot Aaron a wink. "But I do my best."

"Well, Morgan says he'd be lost without you, so you must be doing something right," Dottie cooed, patting her hand. She turned to Aaron, beaming. "But I doubt you came to listen to me prattle on. What can I do for you kiddos?"

Aaron leaned forward, folding his hands together on the table. "Well... to be perfectly honest, Miss Dillons—"

"Please, dear, call me Dottie."

"Dottie," Aaron said with a smile. "I'm..." He blew a breath through tight lips. "I'm planning to propose to Morgan."

"Oh!" Dottie squealed, holding her hands to her cheeks with wide eyes. "Oh ho-ho-ho, how *lovely!* Congratulations!"

"Thank you." Aaron nodded, beaming. "I could buy him any engagement ring that any jeweler in the city could make, but... I want to give him something one of a kind and..."

Dottie's brows lifted slowly as she searched his face. "You seek the Dusk Star, don't you?"

Aaron's jaw dropped as he stammered, "I... yes, that's... *exactly* why we're here. I know you worked at the museum while it was still on exhibit. Do you have any idea what happened to it?"

The woman pursed her lips, turning to stare out the dust-coated window. Her eyes grew dark, glassing over. "I could tell you what I told the authorities..." She reached for her chest, clutching something beneath her blouse. "I could tell you about Mister Barton, the former curator who cared nothing for the preservation of our dwindling history until it benefited him. How I overheard a conversation one night when he thought I'd left for the day and how I learned he intended to steal the jewel after purchasing a one-way caravan ticket to Gavencia."

"It *was* the curator then..." Daphne breathed. "Why cover it up? Why make him disappear as if he had succeeded?"

Dottie rounded on Daphne with shock all over her face. "You know? You know that he... died?"

"We put the pieces together," Aaron said quietly, nodding. "Though, nothing confirms it was his body that went missing from the crime scene. To any outside observer, it was just another of the Harlequins."

A wry chuckle left Dottie's throat as she shook her head. "The Harlequins... Barton's lackeys."

"They were *Barton's* men?" Aaron gasped.

Dottie nodded. "His fences. I'd see one of them, Collins, I think his name was, in the museum lobby on occasion. Always after an exhibit was mysteriously swapped out for another, and the pieces carted across the city to Barton's storage facility."

"The whole museum was his front," Daphne said, laughing derisively. "Fucking hells, this city."

"No respect for the past," Dottie sighed. She jutted her head to gesture over Aaron's shoulder into the living room. "I asked Morgan to procure that vase for me several years ago when the last curator left, afraid that someone else would eventually step in to treat those artifacts the same as Barton had."

Aaron turned in his seat to follow her gaze, glimpsing an elegant white and blue piece of pottery that was easily several centuries out of its time.

"It was nothing special," Dottie said, smiling, "but I took a shine to it back in the 60s, and I couldn't bear the thought of it vanishing one day like so many other precious artifacts had."

"Huh..." Daphne breathed, turning to Aaron. "Wonder why he kept me in the dark about it."

"Oh," Dottie laughed, clutching her chest. "He said you'd never let him forget it if you knew he'd done the job for free. Didn't want you thinking he'd gone soft for a little old lady like me."

Aaron laughed so hard he nearly fell out of his chair, clutching his stomach. "Oh my gods."

"Typical," Daphne chuckled.

"Don't tell him I told you," Dottie snickered. Brushing the hair off the back of her neck, she undid the clasp of a gold chain, coiling it in her fist to withdraw a small key from beneath her blouse. She looked Aaron in the eye, setting the key on the table between them. "Barton planned to use a replica of the stone we sold in the gift shop to replace the original. I waited in that musty storage room for hours, making certain he had left before I did just that."

Aaron took the key between his fingers, smiling at the woman's boldness. "You conned a con artist."

"That I did," she said matter-of-factly, beaming. "I was the one who detailed the exhibits, and the only one in the building other than Barton that had the codes to the alarm systems. I took the Dusk Star, replaced it with the fake, and hid it behind a loose stone in those old tunnels."

"Why tell us?" Aaron asked, searching her eyes. "After all these years? Why not tell Morgan when he went to get the vase for you? He would've given you a fortune for that stone."

"It was never mine to give," Dottie said, shaking her head. "And I know how much trouble sanctioned artifacts can be. I didn't want to burden him any more than I already had."

"But... you're giving it to me now," Aaron cocked an eyebrow with a bemused grin.

"You asked for it." Dottie shrugged, holding out her hand. "If you don't want it—"

"Nope." Aaron pulled his hand back, smiling. "Got a boy to impress."

Dottie chuckled, tucking her hands into her lap. "I have a feeling he would say yes with no ring at all."

"He would," Daphne agreed, leaning back and folding her arms over her chest. "Doesn't stop our gooey romantic here from romancing his ass off."

"Well, then..." Dottie stood, holding out a hand to usher them to the door. "I'd say you have a noble quest to finish. You'll find the outdoor access to the tunnels in an alley behind the convenience store off Sparrow Street. Everyone mistakes it for a sewer access, so they just avoid it."

Aaron opened his arms, smiling wide. "Can I hug you?"

"Oh," Dottie gasped, waddling up to squeeze him around the middle weakly. "Oh, that's quite nice."

Daphne slapped a hand over her mouth to stifle laughter as she backed toward the door.

After Aaron freed himself from the woman's lingering hold, only mildly regretting his decision, they said their goodbyes.

Daphne turned to him on the front step with a lopsided grin. "So, our thief showed up at the drop point with a fake. You realize that she got Barton killed, right?"

"Along with a handful of other thieves." Aaron shrugged, descending the steps. "Dottie didn't pull the trigger, though. They got what they deserved."

"Whoa," Daphne said with an impressed air, "startin' to sound like your fiancé there."

"He's not my fiancé yet, hush," Aaron scoffed, jaunting down the sidewalk with a spring in his step, clutching the key Dottie had given him tight. "And Morgan and I are a lot more alike than you think, Daph. He just readily shows a side I often choose not to."

"Huh..." Daphne chewed her cheek, looking away in thought as she jogged along. "I suppose he does the same when he lets his walls down. Just two sides of the same shiny, gay coin, aren't you?"

Chuckling, Aaron shot her a look over his shoulder. "You have no idea."

That night, Aaron stood in the bedroom, hovering over an open drawer in the large, oak dresser he shared with Morgan. A small wooden box sat in the palm of his hand, his prize sparkling inside with the soft glow of moonlight that trickled in from the window. The Dusk Star, even more radiant than any image had managed to capture, glittered blue, violet and every color in between.

A wrinkled, timeworn note, now clutched in his other hand, had been wrapped around the stone.

"To whoever finds this stone, I beg you, give it the happy ending it deserves."

"She knew the stories..." Aaron muttered under his breath, grinning from ear to ear. "Of course she did." He tucked the note back into the box, locking it up with the key before hiding it beneath a stack of boring, basic white briefs Morgan despised on him, certain it was safe there.

Daphne had begun vetting lapidaries, searching for one with enough skill and discretion to cut the gem down just enough to fit into its future setting, altering its shape so that it would go unrecognized at a glance. Another jeweler in the North District had already taken Aaron's incredibly specific design and was to begin fabricating a palladium band the very next day. All that was left was to find the right time—and the right words.

"Hi, baby," a soft, grunted sigh greeted him as Morgan trudged into the room.

Aaron slid the drawer shut, careful to avoid causing suspicion. "Hey there, beautiful." He held his arms open, letting his boyfriend collapse against his chest. "Rough day?"

"Just... *long*," Morgan groaned. "I get we need to keep an eye out for the splintered covens, but *talking* about it isn't going to accomplish shit. I feel like I'm just there to put everyone at ease."

"That's part of the job, sweetheart," Aaron chuckled, kissing his hair.

"I get that, I do," Morgan said, burying his face in the crook of Aaron's neck. "And I'm partly to blame. It wouldn't be such a big deal that they escaped the Council's custody if we'd made them sign that contract."

Aaron ushered his face upward with one hand on his cheek. "Do you regret—"

"No," Morgan interrupted. "Never. I'm never hiding again, Aaron."

Leaning in, Aaron caught his mouth in a kiss, gently parting his lips with his tongue. Morgan hummed, melting against him, letting the day's tension unravel from his muscles. Aaron pulled away, smiling as he squeezed his witch tighter. "The stars and the moon, visible in broad daylight."

Beneath the denim of Morgan's jeans, Aaron felt a sharp twitch. He chuckled, dipping forward to peck his lips.

"Was... that *not* what you were trying to do?" Morgan asked, eyes flitting between Aaron's face and his own crotch. "It's like you aren't aware how your pretty words affect my body or something."

"Oh, I'm well aware," Aaron growled through a smile. He wrapped both arms around Morgan's back, spinning around to drop him onto the bed.

Morgan giggled beneath him, sticking out his tongue between his teeth. Before Aaron could close the space to his lips again, Morgan put a hand on his chest, holding him back. "Wait!"

Aaron cocked his head, furrowing his brow.

"How'd your investigation go?"

Rolling his eyes, Aaron laughed breathlessly, "You're interrupting foreplay to ask about my day?"

"*Yes*," Morgan said sharply, giving his chest a gentle push. "Because if I don't ask now, I won't have the strength when you're done with me, and I'm not letting you off the hook that easy, Pendragon."

Still chuckling, Aaron gave him a shrug. "Mission accomplished."

"Just like that?"

"Yep," Aaron said smugly. "Turns out it was the curator's body. We think he was paying hush money to the city so he could keep fencing valuables from the museum. He got set up in the end, though. His own thugs took him out."

"Oh, how sad." Morgan feigned sorrow, jutting out his bottom lip with a pout.

"Right? Anyway, Daph shot off an anonymous tip to one of our people. Doubt it will cause much of a stir when it hits the news, but at least it's out there."

"How'd you figure it out?"

"Oh." Aaron's lips curled into a smirk. "We caught up with your friend, Dottie."

Morgan's eyes narrowed.

"She told us *all* your dirty little secrets."

"That's *so* interesting," Morgan droned, reaching down to unbutton Aaron's pants. "But my curiosity is sated now, and I would like to play with your dick, if you don't mind."

Aaron leaned in, hardly containing his laughter. "All about how even before you got your memories back, you were still just a squishy little—"

"Aaron Oliver Jones, shut your mouth and give me your cock," Morgan snapped, grabbing the back of his head to crush their lips together.

Aaron snickered uncontrollably into the kiss, falling into his witch. His future.

His forever.

//ARCHIVED/ECHM.ECNET/EXHIBITS

The Dusk Star

It is with great pride that the Etna City Historical Museum welcomes the famed Alexandrite, The Dusk Star, to our collection.

A jewel with a bloody history, this magnificent stone's first owner was believed to be a British regent during the War of Vorunir. Bequeathed by none other than a witch, the details surrounding its nature have been

Read more ⌄

An optimal summer setting for the climate generators and a deal struck between our heroes.

Although, Aaron had no idea it would cost him a piggyback ride.

Originally released on my birthday, this heartwarming trip to the beach still brings me joy.

This short was released on May 17th, 2024

Close to Forever

05.17.204 UI

Dulcet tones of pink and gold invaded the twilight sky. Car horns blazed. People on their way to begin their day trickled out onto the sidewalks, clutching coffees and cheap pastries as they went.

Morgan's stomach rumbled from the parapet at the thought of baked goods. He placed an empty mug on the ledge beside him, torn between the urge to get more coffee and the view. The skyline mesmerized and inspired him every morning, even as the city and life within it remained entirely the same.

"Morning, sweetheart," a warm voice yawned over the screech of the access door.

"Hey, baby." Morgan turned, beaming at the only sight that could hold his gaze more firmly than his ritual sunrise. "Sorry. You were sleeping so well. I didn't want to wake you."

"I knew exactly where to find you." Aaron leaned down, pecking his lips with a chuckle. He passed Morgan a plate containing a single, gargantuan cinnamon roll, heaping with cream cheese frosting, along with another cup of coffee.

"Oh." Morgan's eyes lit up as the glorious scent of cinnamon filled his nose. "Best. Boyfriend. Ever."

Aaron laughed, moving the empty mug to sit beside him. "Sweets were always the way to your heart. Glad that hasn't changed. So many more options to butter you up with here."

Morgan's brow furrowed as he stuffed his face. "Whud you buddering me up for?"

Aaron gave him a sideways grin, folding his hands in his lap and swinging his feet. "Well... the climate gens are set to their optimal summer program today. I thought... maybe we could take advantage?"

Morgan raised one eyebrow, swallowing his mouthful. "You want to go *swimming*."

"Bingo." Aaron grinned from ear to ear.

"In that nasty ass water on the boardwalk," Morgan scoffed, "instead of the perfectly, magically cleaned pool in the Manor?"

"Come on, babe!" Aaron whined. "I haven't been to the beach since Camelot—"

"And look how big and strong you grew up from all the no diseases you got."

"And we used to have so much fun going to the ocean together back home."

"You mean before humanity reached the Industrial Revolution, conceived the harebrained notion of capitalism and got all trash happy?"

Then his boyfriend whipped out his secret weapon. His power move. Morgan's greatest weakness—the puppy dog eyes. "*Please?*"

"Godsdammit, Aaron." Morgan averted his gaze, already melting on the inside.

"I know you've already got some kind of spell cooking in that gorgeous head of yours to keep the water clean while we swim."

"Flattery on top of those eyes? Really?"

"And I already bought some *very* skimpy swimwear for us."

Morgan coughed on his pastry. Aaron scooted close, patting his back with a soft giggle. When Morgan could breathe again he asked, "*How* skimpy?"

Aaron grinned. "Low cut. Box style. Legs cut above my junk."

"Blue?"

"Duh."

"Ugh." Morgan threw his head back, caving entirely. "Deal."

Shane patted his pockets, fishing out the handheld carving tool Morgan used for his bullets. "Right here."

Morgan stood, holding out the rock. "Stack *purify* and *magnify* in succession, then contain it in a repeating series of *break, dissolve* and *scatter*. The magic won't extend more than half a kilometer or so, but it should do the trick."

"Aww..." Shane groaned, taking the stone. "Come on. We're on vacation and I still gotta work on my runes?"

Morgan rolled his eyes, strutting away from the man. "I'm going easy on you, believe me. Should've seen the shit Merlin made me do."

"It's true," Aaron said with a grin, watching his gorgeous witch's backside. "Once he had to keep the entire string ensemble playing during our yearly meet with the surrounding kingdoms, glamour it to look like there were people playing them so that my father didn't notice, all the while entertaining at least ten of the attending ladies with a dance."

Shane raised an eyebrow, glancing back and forth between him and Morgan. "Sounds like a breeze for Morgan."

"*Now*, sure." Aaron laughed, walking over to grab the cooler before following his boyfriend. "But he was only eight."

Thirty minutes later, the beach was beginning to look like a summer dream. Morgan and Aaron worked on setting up a long net, raised high on two poles for a game Aaron wanted to play. Both had tossed their shirts aside, now wearing nothing but the swimwear Aaron had bought for them. Their efforts had drawn a small crowd along the boardwalk, people staring and pointing from up above.

Gwen, Lance, Percy and Wain all poured out of the blac conversion van, each of them dressed for a swim. Percy r through the sand, brushing a strawberry blond curl out of

Morgan leaned down, whispering against his ear. "Be a good horsey now, and I'll ride you without the trunks later."

Aaron sighed, leaning back to kiss him quickly. "Like you weren't going to anyway."

"Less talking, more moving, steed!" Morgan leaned down to smack his ass.

Aaron lunged along the surf, kicking up sand as they went. "I could totally just dive into the water right now, you know."

Morgan's grip on him tightened. "I will turn you into an actual horse, Aaron Oliver Jones. Don't you dare!"

"You would never," Aaron huffed, spinning around to run back along the shoreline.

"Nah," Morgan chuckled, hugging him from behind. "I like this shape, and certain parts of you are already pretty horse-like."

"In exactly what ways am I—" Aaron snapped, then his face went blank. "*Oh.*"

Morgan snickered, peppering his cheek with kisses. "So pretty."

"Hey, guys?" Gwen shouted across the way from a lounge chair, sprawled out beneath an umbrella. "We've got company."

Both Aaron and Morgan's heads snapped in the direction she waved her hand, sighting Daphne and Lance deep in conversation with a crowd that had gathered at the edge of the beach. Morgan climbed off Aaron, taking his hand to drag him through the sand.

"Everything alright here?" Aaron called over.

Daphne glanced back at them, then turned to the person she'd been speaking with. "Uh, yeah, it's just..."

"They're wondering if they can join us." Lance shot them a smile, arms crossed over his bare chest.

Daphne blew out a breath, holding up a finger to the crowd before pacing over. "It's not just that..."

Morgan's brow furrowed, shooting the small mass of people a look. "What is it?"

She sighed, adjusting one of the straps of her bright yellow bikini. "They recognize the two of you after all the news coverage from Abernathy and Aaron leaving the force, and..."

"They're worried Morgan is going to set them on fire?" Aaron grinned at him.

"Rude."

"I mean... yeah, kinda." Daphne gave him an apologetic smile.

"What?!" Morgan gasped, jaw hanging. "I've never attacked random civilians!"

"Sweetie, they don't know what to believe, okay?" Daphne placed a hand on his shoulder. "Between the police reports and Esotech's statements, they're confused, but..."

"But what?" Morgan growled.

"But they're still here, sweetheart," Aaron said, pulling his hand to his lips to kiss his knuckles. "Look at them."

Morgan followed his gaze, locking eyes with a multitude of curious stares. Some looked away, pretending they had been staring anywhere else. Others actually smiled, and he could've sworn one of them almost waved before dropping their hand to scratch their chin.

"They're questioning the lies, Morgan," Aaron continued, tucking a hand around his waist. "They see us here, laughing and trying to make this place better... and they're asking if they can be a part of it."

Morgan bit his lip, fighting back his gut instincts. With a deep breath, he released Aaron's hand, and moved toward the crowd. Lancelot turned to him as he approached, nodded once, and stepped to the side.

"Uh..." Morgan breathed, looking over the crowd. There were a few couples that were out enjoying the weather together, just as he and Aaron were. One large family that looked as if they'd just come down from the boardwalk carried prizes from the arcade, and several people hovered further back, standing on their tiptoes to look over the rest. Morgan cleared his throat. "First of all, I'm not going to harm any of you so long as you're not here to cause us trouble."

"Did you really bewitch Aaron to be your boyfriend?" one of them shouted.

"What?" Morgan sputtered. "No! Who even said that?"

"Some tabloid," an older gentleman who looked vaguely familiar croaked, rolling his eyes at the one who had asked the question. "Don't listen to 'em. Morgan's the good sorta witch. He saved Aaron's keester."

"Mister Reynolds?" Aaron called over, jogging up to Morgan's side.

"Ey, muh boy!" The man beamed at him. "Mighty fine work you and your friends are doin' here."

Aaron slung one arm over Morgan's shoulders, pecking his cheek with a kiss. "Nah, it's all them. I'm just here to observe... and give piggyback rides, apparently."

"So, can we play in the water?" one of the children squealed. "It's so hot!"

"I've never been in the ocean before!"

Morgan turned to Shane where he worked closer to the parked vehicles, chewing his lip as he carved delicate patterns into the stone. "How's it coming, Shane?"

Shane swatted his palm over the surface of the rock, dusting away debris. He cocked his head, carefully examining his runes as Morgan drew near. "You tell me, boss."

Taking the stone, Morgan meticulously appraised his newest apprentice's work, tracing the carvings with his fingertips. His brows arched as he reached the final sequence of runes, finding no errors. "Damn. That's some solid engraving."

"Really?" Shane gasped, a crack in his voice.

"It's perfect, Shane." Morgan nodded, bouncing the stone in his palm. "Now for the magic."

The entire crowd gathered on the beach as those with magic stood at the shoreline, surrounding Morgan on all sides. He held the stone aloft in both hands, calling his own power to the surface. His eyes lit violet, and the patterns upon the stone began to pulse. "Daph, you're up."

Daphne touched her fingertips to the stone, irises shining as her golden magic took its place alongside Morgan's.

"Frey..." Morgan nodded to the fairy.

Frey added their own rose hue to the runes, eyes glittering pink.

"Lucas, your turn."

The House Balen witch reached out, complimenting House Fell's colors with a vivid splash of sunset orange.

"Now you, baby." Morgan turned to Aaron beside him.

"What... how do I—" Aaron stammered, holding out his hand. "I can't use it outside of runes, sweetheart."

Morgan chuckled. "These *are* runes. They're just not attached to you. Touch the surface. Think of what we need this magic to do, and push just like you do in battle to release your spells."

Aaron placed his fingers on the stone. Morgan felt the familiar tug in his chest, the sensation of sharing his power with the one he loved most, and bright cobalt blue slipped into the carvings.

"Whoa," Aaron breathed. "I didn't know it could act beyond my own body."

Morgan smiled brightly at him. "When we're working together, it can. Think of it like closing the loop. You and I pull from the same source—me. I started the infusion, you ended it."

"Which should allow this rock here to do its job for a ridiculously long time," Daphne said.

"Like magical bookends?" Aaron mused.

Everyone laughed. "If that helps," Morgan snickered. He felt resistance against his magic and lowered the stone. "That should do it."

The others withdrew their hands, and Morgan passed the glowing stone to Aaron. "Double up on *force*, add *magnify*, and chuck this thing as far as you can."

"Chuck it?" Aaron took the stone in both hands, glancing around. "Where?"

Morgan belted a laugh. "Where do you think?" He pointed straight out into the ocean.

"Oh..." Aaron shot him a lopsided grin, shifting the rock to tap at his runes. "I got this." He took several steps back, twirling his right arm with the stone held tight. His chest rose with a deep inhale, and he let it out, racing toward the water. A grunt left his throat as he hurled the stone, a pulse of blue propelling it with magical intent as it left his grip.

People cheered from behind, oohing and aahing at his performance. The shine of the runes etched upon the stone blinked brightly against the blue sky as it sailed away, nearly vanishing from sight before plummeting into the depths.

Morgan moved to Aaron's side, eyes fixed on the ocean. "That was hot."

Daphne chuckled, lacing her fingers into Shane's hand as he pulled up behind her. "I feel like he could clip his toenails, and you'd say it was hot."

Morgan shot her a grimace. "No. No, I think we found the line. Well done."

Aaron huffed a laugh, pulling him into his arms. "Did it work?" he whispered, staring out into the water.

"Just wait," Morgan uttered, resting his head back on Aaron's shoulder.

The waves rolled in and out over their feet. Gwen and Lance sidled up next to them, followed by Wain as Percy went to stand beside Lucas.

"Any second now..." Morgan breathed, a smirk gracing his lips.

A flash of light raced through the water. Ripples pulsed across the surface, cascading through the oncoming waves, and the ocean began to glow as far as the eye could see.

"Voila." Morgan clapped his hands together. "That should keep the area sanitary for at least a few decades."

"It won't hurt us?" one of their audience asked breathlessly. "The magic, I mean. Is it safe?"

Morgan rolled his eyes, smiling. "Its intent is to keep the water clean. It's as safe as an ocean can be, I promise you."

Everyone stared, glancing between Morgan and the ocean as the light of their spell dimmed away. Aaron chuckled, jabbing a thumb over his shoulder. "Well? Go on, then. Get in there."

The people raced out into the water, laughing, yelling, and kicking up sand in their wake. Daphne charged in after Shane, squealing with delight as she leapt on top of him, tackling him into the water. Frey dipped a toe in, pursing their lips before practically throwing themself into the waves. Gwen dragged Lance out next, followed closely by Wain, Percy and Lucas.

Their friends shouted and cheered, splashing each other and diving beneath the surface to escape retaliation. Morgan's face lit with joy, watching them play.

"*Fy cariad...*" Aaron cooed, holding out a hand as he stepped backward into the water.

"Oof. Déjà vu." Morgan blinked the sunlight out of his eyes, shaking his head. "*Major* déjà vu."

Aaron laughed, taking Morgan's hand to pull him out into the water. When the waves reached their navels, Aaron pulled him to his chest, crushing their lips together. Morgan hummed with delight, lazily flitting his eyes open when Aaron broke the kiss.

"You just gave the city an actual beach," Aaron whispered, running a thumb along Morgan's jaw. "You're amazing, you know that?"

"*We* did this," Morgan said airily, searching his eyes. "You wanted to go swimming. What else was I going to do?"

"I don't know." Aaron shrugged, gazing out to the horizon. "I thought maybe you'd cast some protection spells or just push the filth further out into the ocean while we were here. I guess... I didn't expect something so... *permanent.*"

A giggle bubbled through Morgan's lips. He shook his head, smiling wide. "Every single thing I do for you..." He poked Aaron in the chest, right over his heart. "...will always be as close to forever as I can get."

Etna City Pride.

I had to stop and imagine if such a celebration would exist in my world. As Morgan said, humanity continues to fall short even after a seventeen century long nap. So, of course, a reminder of love and community would still be desperately needed.

Never forget that you are loved, that you belong, and that the world is a better place with you in it.

This short was released on June 28th, 2024

The Riot of Lights

06.20.204 UI

Color everywhere. Flags and banners. Pulsating lights and hails of confetti sailing through the darkening sky. If Etna was the neon city and Beat Street the heart, then that heart had grown full to bursting.

People laughed and cheered, dancing in the open road and leaping into the air with fists raised high. Energetic music of vocals carried on an electric symphony rang out over the crowd, bouncing between buildings and down alleys, enveloping every patron, heart, body and soul.

And in bright letters above a ticketed gate, flashed the words *Etna City's 50th Annual Riot of Lights Celebration.*

Morgan couldn't help the smile that lit his face, taking in the atmosphere. His grin stretched as Aaron walked forward to pay for their entire group, reveling in the sight of his gorgeous frame beneath a baggy tank top bearing a graffitied crown—The Majesty's logo—in pink, purple and blue.

Not to mention the new look he'd adopted to add a little lawbreaking edge to perfection.

Aaron's golden hair, sparkling in the evening sun, had been shaved close on either side of his head, decorated with three sharp lines above his ears. And the piercings—dear *gods*, the piercings—a row of three silver hoops up his right ear that made Morgan's blood run hot.

His boyfriend glanced back at him, shooting a wink as he held his hand above the scanner.

Aaron's gaze raked over Morgan's chest adorned with a rainbow crown on a white tee cropped above his navel, before trailing down to his waist where a white leather belt smattered in color held tight jeans in place. Given permission to show off, Morgan dove at the opportunity considering the climate generators were at their highest temperature settings, heat still lingering in the late afternoon.

Quite a few eyes had already loitered on his figure other than his boyfriend's, but neither he nor Aaron truly minded. They'd received so much media attention over the last few months—the battle in the wastes, the scandal that was an ECPD officer leaving the force and joining a coven, constant coverage of them combatting the rifts, and even a few light-hearted pieces featuring the two of them as a couple—as soon as whoever was gawking realized who they were staring at, their eyes instantly snapped away.

And honestly, resoundingly and absolutely—none of them stood a chance.

"Dude, this is so *luxe!*" Shane shouted, bobbing and swaying, wearing a bright, tie-dyed T-shirt in pink, blue and yellow as all members of House Fell passed through the barricades sectioning the festival off from traffic. "How have I never been to this before?! It's like a big, gay party in the street!"

"Uh..." Gwen cocked her head with a confused grin, leaning into Lance. "Yeah, that's exactly what it is, Shane. Aaron and I have been coming every year since we met."

"It's more than a *party*," Aaron scoffed reaching out for Morgan's hand to lead them all deeper into the festival. "Etna might be a safe place for queer folk, but the world tends to forget that it wasn't always a welcome notion. Hells, back home, we could have never walked around town doing this." He lifted their joined hands to his lips, kissing Morgan's knuckles.

"Seriously?" Shane raised a brow. "I can't imagine a world where you two aren't touching twenty-four seven."

"Shut up," Morgan chuckled. "It wasn't safe. Even after he took the throne, we had no idea who might cause us problems."

Aaron nodded, stopping in front of a pop-up bar on the sidewalk. "One amber and one... hmm..." He studied the menu, scrawled out in all colors of the rainbow on a white board. "Nothing hard on the list, babe."

"Two ambers." Morgan gave the attendant a soft smile, jabbing a thumb over his shoulder at their friends. "And whatever this lot is having."

The others called out their orders as Aaron grabbed the two plastic cups the bartender placed on the counter, passing one to Morgan with a swig of his own. "But yeah, we kept our affections within the castle for the most part. For our own peace of mind, if nothing else."

"That's stupid," Shane growled, snatching up his own cup and glaring into its contents. "If a fucking *king* isn't allowed to hold hands with the person they love, then who is?"

Aaron laughed derisively. "I was *allowed*. I mean, shit, one of the first decrees we made was to abolish my father's discrimination laws. Morgan and I agreed though, when it came to our relationship, that was about us. No one else."

"But..." Frey frowned, licking their lips that had been stained red from a fruity, non-alcoholic beverage. They glanced down at Aaron and Morgan's joined hands before looking Morgan in the eyes. "You're holding hands now. Why is it different?"

"Because we know that *here*..." Morgan turned his head, smiling as he took in the crowd. "No one is going to think twice about it. Whenever we chose to do something that any other couple might do naturally and without thinking in a public space, it's sort of like an alarm would go off in our heads."

"Danger!" Daphne said in a deep and goofy voice. "Potential for bigoted assholes!"

Morgan laughed. "Yeah, pretty much. And then we'd have to decide-"

"Do we keep touching despite the concern?" Aaron interjected. "Or do we just enjoy our time together without having to worry?"

"We told you all the time we would've gone into town with you guys," Percy said with a shrug. "No one would've dared to even give you a dirty look."

"We know that, Perce," Morgan said before kicking back the rest of his drink. "And we love you for it, but then it was no longer about *us*. The moment we pressed on, it became bigger. As if we were making a statement to everyone around us instead of a simple, 'Hey, you're mine, and I'm yours, hold this.'"

Aaron laughed heartily, taking his cup and placing it back on the counter alongside his own. "Everything we did was always bigger than us. We had to keep some things to ourselves."

"Not here though," Morgan sighed happily, moving into Aaron's space. "Not ever again."

"Well, let's keep *some* things to ourselves," Aaron chuckled, wrapping a hand around the bare skin of his lower back. "You're already half on display for all these people. The rest is *mine*."

"Greedy boy," Morgan giggled, draping both arms over his shoulders and leaning in.

"With you?" Aaron pulled him right up against his chest, whispering against his lips. "Always."

His lips met Morgan's, sticky, sweet and delicious with a gentle hum. Morgan let himself sink into the kiss, tightening his embrace as the raucous cheer surrounding them faded to a dull roar. When the world fell away like this, every moment together was theirs and only theirs, no matter the audience. With Aaron, all else was forgotten.

"Oh my gods, it *is* them!" An unhinged squeal sent them plummeting back to reality. "I told you!"

"Well, Morgan is wearing *rainbows!* I wasn't sure!" another voice shouted.

"Morgan! Aaron! Can we get a picture with you?!"

"What's happening?" Morgan blinked his eyes open, head still buzzing from his hit of Aaron. "Why do those awful noises sound like our names? Make it stop."

"I think you have fans, sweetie," Daphne said, holding a hand over her lips to hide a smile. She leaned into Shane, shaking her head. "Holding hands is one thing, but if you two are gonna suck face in public, people are going to stare regardless of what century we're in."

Sure enough, a small crowd had pressed in around them, smiling and waving, tapping at their temples to take pictures.

"Kiss him again! That was *hot!*"

"Can I join House Fell?! I'll show you *both* some magic!"

"Well, this was fun," Morgan droned, sulking sideways into Aaron. "Time to go home."

Aaron shook with silent laughter, grabbing him around the waist to pull him back to his chest. "You'll be okay, sweetheart. This is the good kind of attention."

"No such thing." Morgan rolled his eyes, forcing a smile for those taking pictures. "Unless it's your attention, I don't want it."

"Said the guy that's been on the news regularly for the past five and a half years," Shane snickered.

"Hated it, still hate it, and hate you too, bitch," Morgan said, still grinning uncomfortably.

"Lies," Shane laughed.

Aaron kissed his cheek, giving him a squeeze. "You know perfectly well how to handle being in the public eye, babe. We've done it before, and I have a feeling it's only going to become more common from here on out. Just lean into it with me and enjoy the ride."

Morgan's brows raised, wearing a goofy grin.

Aaron snorted, giving him a playful shove. "You know what I meant. Stop that."

"Never," Morgan snickered.

Giving in and indulging the paparazzi had opened a door, and Aaron wasn't certain it should be left ajar. He knew they were bound to be singled out eventually, given his boyfriend's penchant for calling attention to himself and the media's incessant coverage of their every move. What he hadn't expected was the total lack of animosity toward them.

People greeted them everywhere they went, offering to buy them drinks and showering them with adoration. Despite his very vocal reservations, Morgan had been handling their fans quite well for the past few hours, taking pictures, holding conversations, and even making a connection with the fashion magazine, Avante.

Aaron laughed silently as Morgan leaned into his side, posing for a few shots for the magazine's Pride feature.

"What's so funny?" Morgan muttered.

"Just remembering our conversation about Avante on our first date here." He smiled wide, wrapping a hand around Morgan's waist.

"Ah, yes," Morgan chuckled, "When you interrupted the bearing of my soul to *flirt*."

"Don't play with me, Morgan Fell," Aaron smacked a kiss on his cheek. "You'd take even my worst one-liners over revealing your dark secrets any day."

Morgan laughed. "True."

"Alright, fellas," the cameraman shouted over, "give me your sexiest pose! Think runway model for me!"

Morgan rolled his eyes, breathing a chuckle as he put both hands behind his head, cocking his head to the side and popping his hip. Aaron blanked completely. "Uh..."

"You okay, baby?" Morgan teased. "Too much attention for you?"

"I... how do I..."

"Just give them a wink or something," Morgan snickered. "Lift up your shirt. Show some skin."

Aaron shot him a pout. "Not everyone is as shameless as you."

"Everything alright?" the cameraman called.

Aaron groaned, his cheeks flushing. Shoving down his nerves, he pulled Morgan to his side. He lifted his shirt to give them a good view of his hard-earned abs, winked, and, for some reason, stuck out his tongue. It seemed to do the trick, at least.

"Yes! Good!" the man cheered, tapping away. "Pull Morgan closer for me, Aaron! Yes, perfect!"

"Why the tongue?" Morgan asked through poorly veiled amusement.

"Shut up. I hate you." Aaron snapped, returning to his ridiculous pose.

A loudspeaker boomed through the street, causing everyone to turn toward the sound. "Ladies, gentleman, and gender-unburdened—"

"That's a wrap, fellas!" The cameraman gave them a thumbs-up. "Showtime!"

"What's up?" Morgan asked, dropping his hands as he whipped his head around, searching the street.

"The main event," Aaron said with a grin, pulling him back onto the sidewalk.

"Please make way for our annual parade, led by none other than our fabulous light guard—The Syndicate Spectral!"

The crowd parted, joining them on the sidewalk to reveal a whirl of lights parading down the street. Dancers flipped and twirled in sync with one another, flailing lights held in their hands, flashing and spiraling outfits riddled with pulsating color.

"Whoa..." Morgan's eyes widened at the spectacle. "That's fucking *cool*."

"Right?!" Aaron cheered, wrapping him up in his arms from behind. "I hope the others are watching. You see them anywhere?"

Morgan scanned the crowd, shaking his head. "I'm sure they heard the announcement. We'll catch up with them later."

"And marching right behind them, we have Etna City University's Future Leaders program! Give them a cheer, Etna! This celebration couldn't have come together without their help! These amazing youths made your festival shine!"

A roar filled the streets, laden with whistling and cheers. Aaron shouted over Morgan's shoulder, giving him a start. "Sorry, babe," he whispered in his ear, giving him a gentle squeeze.

Morgan sank back into him with a smile. "I love how much you love this."

Aaron kissed his cheek, nuzzling into the crook of his neck. "Are you having fun?"

"I am," Morgan said, resting his head on Aaron's. "Seriously, it's... uplifting to see that humanity has progressed in *some* ways since home at least."

"It is," Aaron breathed. "It was a long road though, and there are still people that refuse to understand, even if they're quieter about it."

Morgan sighed with a nod. "The fight's never really over, is it?"

"No," Aaron agreed. "But that's life isn't it? We'll always have to fight for what matters. If not for ourselves, then for others who can't fend for themselves. People like you and me, like Daphne, Shane, and even Frey—though they may not really know how difficult the world can be yet—we know better than most that there will always be a reason to fight. That doesn't mean we don't stop and celebrate what we have along the way."

With a smile, Morgan leaned back to meet his eyes. "I'll always celebrate you."

Aaron laughed softly, pressing a quick kiss to his lips. "I know. And I know our lives are chaotic. I know there is constantly something new to surmount, but as long as I'm doing it with you and our friends, our family, then I'm forever grateful for the madness that brought us here. Even the bad parts."

"Oh, I don't know if I'd go *that* far," Morgan laughed, suddenly interrupted by another kiss. "Me too. I love you, and I love our crazy life. Maybe one day we'll be able to do something that mildly resembles settling down."

The notion shot Aaron's thoughts back to the Manor. Glittering hues of blue and purple, dancing within a trillion-cut gemstone and wrapped in a gorgeous silver band. The hard-won trophy he and Daphne had been scheming for since Solstice, finally ready to make a promise of forever with.

"Yeah," he whispered, holding his witch impossibly closer. "One day."

With the end of the parade, House Fell had reconvened at the gate, exhausted, returning home to scatter themselves over the Manor rooftop. Morgan sank happily into Aaron as they lounged on the parapet, drinking and staring out to where the party continued, lighting the skyline even brighter than usual.

The night air nipped at the skin below his top, and he zipped an oversized blue hoodie of his boyfriend's up to his chest.

"Why are we all up here again?" Gawain shivered, rubbing his arms.

Morgan wafted a hand through the air, sending a warm pulse across the space. "To watch the closing ceremony, Wain."

"How are we meant to do that from here?" he asked, furrowing his brow.

"Just watch," Aaron assured him.

Morgan smiled, nestling into his side, when the night exploded in color. Dazzling flares in every shade danced across the sky, popping and cracking through the air, sending cascades of light downward toward the city as they sparkled away. Everyone gasped, oohing and aahing with each burst.

"*Wooooow...*" Frey whispered, standing on their tiptoes and bouncing with delight.

"What in the devil..." Lance breathed, leaning forward. "Is that... magic?"

"Technically," Aaron said, nodding as he draped an arm over Morgan's shoulders. "They're the modern equivalent of fireworks, created with rune-tech so they don't damage the environment worse than it already is. Once upon a time they were one hell of a lot louder and made with actual gunpowder."

"You know an alchemist actually invented them trying to find immortality?" Morgan mused, watching the display with wide eyes.

"I don't..." Shane muttered, half paying attention to his ravings. "How would the two even relate? I feel like you'd find the exact opposite. Big boom. Big dead."

Daphne chuckled at his side. "I mean... we've seen exactly what brand of crazy people get up to looking for power of any kind."

"True story," Gwen said, clinking her bottle with Daphne's.

Silence fell over the rooftop as they all stared in awe. Lance stroked Gwen's hair while she rested her head on his lap. Daphne's cheek was on Shane's shoulder, their hands interlaced as they spoke in hushed whispers. Percy and Wain leaned against the wall, shoulders pressed together for warmth. Frey danced along the parapet, adding nothing but whimsy to an already magical night.

The fireworks ended in a blaze of glory, scattering light so wide that not a single corner of the horizon was left unpainted. One by one, the others stood to their feet, uttering their goodnights before striding to the access door, until only Morgan and Aaron remained.

"Thank you," Morgan whispered, dropping his head onto Aaron's shoulder.

"For what, *fy cariad?*"

"Showing me something wonderful," he uttered. "Reminding me once again that we're not alone."

Aaron smiled, beautiful and far more stunning than any shower of light across the sky. "You're so very welcome, my sweet boy. I'm glad you had a good time." He leaned closer, catching his lips.

Morgan melted into the kiss. His hands slid over Aaron's chest, threading their way beneath the cut shoulders of his shirt. The muscles in his back rolled beneath Morgan's fingers as he shifted, pulling him down to the ground. They laughed into the kiss as they fell backward onto the cement, Morgan straddling Aaron's hips.

"Shall we go to bed?" Aaron muttered against his lips.

Morgan sat up, grinning wickedly as he held him in place with his palms against his chest. "Nope."

Aaron cocked his head with a questioning look. "But..." He waved a hand at the cement behind his head. "Ow."

Shrugging off his hoodie, Morgan rolled it into a tight ball. He leaned down, tucking it beneath Aaron's head and giving him another quick kiss. "There. Now relax and let me live out a fantasy."

Aaron's eyes popped. "What fantasy would that be exactly?"

In answer to his question, Morgan snaked a hand between their bodies, finding his boyfriend's half-hard cock beneath the denim, giving it a firm squeeze. Aaron's breath hitched, a grin spreading over his face to wash away any lingering confusion.

"The light pollution might hinder our view up here," Morgan teased, sliding down his body, "but I can still make you see *stars*."

He brought his face level with Aaron's hips, unfastening his jeans. A rattled breath left his boyfriend's lips as he kissed along the swelling outline in his briefs. Sinking back onto his knees, he gave a tug on the waistband, letting Aaron's dick slap against his belly. His grin stretched, eyes flitting between those bright blue eyes, blown wide in the dark, and that gorgeous length befitting a man born into royalty.

Morgan leaned in, taking him in one hand to kiss softly at the crown, dragging his lips down the shaft to the base. Aaron's head fell back onto the makeshift pillow, chest rising and falling faster with every taunting movement. "You're gonna... have to heal your knees later, sweetheart."

"Hush," Morgan whispered, running a hand up Aaron's waist through the fine hairs there, tracing the cut valleys of his stomach with his fingertips. "I'll wear the bruises with pride, just like any others you've ever left with your lips." He dropped his head, taking him all the way to the back of his throat.

Aaron gasped a laugh, staring up to the sky with hooded eyes. Morgan pulled off slightly, wrapping his fingers around the base to work him with both his lips and his fist. Aaron's body gave a shudder beneath the hand roaming his torso. "Fuck... holy fuck, babe."

Hints of bitter sweetness danced over Morgan's tongue, his king already coming undone little by little. The cut of cement into his legs was forgotten, his senses wholly overpowered by desire. He locked eyes with Aaron, veins set ablaze by that look on his face. Lips parted and gasping for breath. Brows pinched together above a desperate stare, begging, pleading to be sent spiraling over the edge.

"Yes..." Aaron whimpered, reaching down to tangle his fist in Morgan's hair. "Yes, my sweet boy. Just like that."

The sky lit up once again, another wave of fireworks filling Aaron's gaze with light. The sound and sight failed miserably to break their connection, neither willing to look away from the other for any view, any glimpse of beauty or wonderous vision this world had to offer.

"Morgan..." Aaron's eyes drifted upward. Muscles along his stomach tightened. His hips jerked upward, slamming his cock deeper into Morgan's throat. "Fuck... Fuck, Morgan..."

"*Come for me, baby,*" Morgan sang into his mind, hollowing his cheeks.

Aaron's jaw dropped to his chest. His fingers clenched over Morgan's scalp, the sting only serving to entangle ecstasy among euphoria with the groan that ripped its way out of Aaron's throat. Warmth and salt washed over Morgan's throat, down his tongue, over and again with every pulse of his release. Aaron held on tight, grounding himself as his entire body convulsed, each spasm visibly taking him apart. "Morgan... Morgan..."

Morgan sat back with a swallow, licking his lips and grinning down at the fruits of his labor—his own beating heart, a gorgeous puddle of a man, heaving shallow breaths in the center of his rooftop.

"Fuck stars..." Aaron rasped, placing a hand over his chest. "Seven hells, I saw whole galaxies, Morgan."

Morgan chuckled, crawling over him to reach his face. He caught his lips, tugging the bottom one gently with his teeth as he pulled away. "*Now* we can go to bed."

Aaron smiled, grabbing both of Morgan's shoulders as he closed the space, kissing him again. "Good. What I have in store for you won't go well up here."

Giggling, Morgan slipped a hand into his pocket, not willing to waste a second with something as mundane as walking, and an anchor whisked them away to make their own fireworks from the comfort of their bed.

//AVANTE.ECNET/JUNE

AVANTE

House Fell stuns with an appearance at the Riot of Lights!

And so we come, not to the end, but the precipice.

The second and final exclusive to Between Once & Forever, seen through the eyes of Morgan's most recent protégé.

Life in Etna City has become so much more than any of our heroes could have imagined, and when plans made fall into place…

…everything will change.

The Second Apprentice

07.05.204 UI

*F*ear—a series of four angled lines, slashed through with another. Begin with the broadest and most encompassing rune, as taught. *Flood*—a circle encompassed by another, the outer shape broken on opposite sides. Give the initial carving a command, then sharpen its focus with *push*—three more lines that curve more as they move outward.

Shane's assignment was to replicate a spell using only runes all on his own, and there was one particular ability he knew Morgan was capable of that he would love to have in his arsenal. Etching the inner circle for his *push* rune, he bit his lip, holding his hand steady. If nothing else ever came of his studies, at least his carving technique had come leaps and bounds over the course of the last eight months.

Since becoming Morgan's second apprentice, Shane had spent more time in his personal little corner of the armory than he had in his own room. He delicately brushed silver shavings from the bangle where it was held tight in a vice at his worktable, assessing his handiwork with his fingertips. "Alright... let's give that a shot."

With a crank of the vice, he plucked the bangle free, slipping it onto his wrist. He trailed his palm over the markings in the silver, willing them to act. The witches in his life often likened the use of their magic to water, flowing through them like the blood in their veins as it heeded their call. For him though, if he really concentrated, he might experience a light trickle.

That was him. One leaky faucet of a witch—the pride and joy of House Fell.

The runes at his wrist glowed a soft white. A gentle ripple of energy enveloped him, moving away slowly. Before he could even decide who to test his creation on, a hiss beneath his worktable had him leaping back. A ball of black fur standing on end darted out from between the legs of the table, snarling and growling.

"Oh, *shit—Glimmer!*"

Claws tore up his leg in the blink of an eye. Vials of glass went flying off the shelf behind him. A stack of books flew from atop the cabinet, and the streak of angry fur vanished.

"*Mother—*" Shane hissed through gritted teeth as he dropped down, pulling up his shredded pant leg to assess the damage. Blood dripped from four deep cuts in his calf. "Yeah... yeah, I deserved that."

"Pulse check!" the unbothered voice of his girlfriend echoed from the door to the main hall.

"I'm fine," Shane groaned, ripping the bangle off his arm to chuck it to the floor. "Could use a quick fix, though."

"Oh, ow!" Daphne jogged around a bookcase, kneeling down at his side. She held a palm over the cuts, eyes glowing gold. "So *you* pissed of the feral creature that just flew through the living room."

"Didn't know she was in here," Shane sighed, running his palm over his mended skin as she pulled away. "Think I overdid it trying to replicate Morgan's intimidation spell."

Daphne patted his shoulder, leaning in to kiss his cheek before standing to retrieve the bangle from the floor. "Oh gods, Shane, *push* after *flood?* Those are synergistic as follow up commands. You're lucky she didn't transform and eat you."

"Okay, but Morgan can literally make entire streets full of people jump out of the way!" Shane whined, pushing his hair out of his face. "That has to take a lot of oomph, right?"

Tossing the bangle on the worktable with a shrug, Daphne sighed, "I think that's got a lot to do with augmenting perception over outright causing a spike of fear. Never really worked out how he does it, but Morgan uses existing forces to his advantage when he can."

Shane pursed his lips, searching the floor in thought. "So, you're saying the fact that the city already harbors an underlying fear toward him gives him an edge?"

"Something like that," Daphne chuckled. "Fat lot of good it's going to do him these days."

"What do you mean?"

"I don't think he's used that spell in months," Daphne said, wafting a hand at the shattered glass on the floor to restore the broken vials. "Probably because it won't evoke the same response in people. Hells, he might summon a fangirl squad if he tried now."

Shane snorted at the mental image.

"It's just a theory," Daphne muttered, giving him a shrug and a sweet smile. "You know how tight-lipped he can be about his own creations."

"You think he'll be upset that I tried to replicate it?" Shane asked with a twinge of guilt.

"Nope," Daphne chimed, bouncing away to the meeting table. "When it comes to witchcraft, imitation is indeed the highest form of flattery. Might be upset you freaked the fuck out of his cat, though."

"I think I've paid for that one," Shane chuckled, eyeing her as she took a seat near the head of the table, tapping her comm. "Are we... do we have a meeting?"

"Uh..." Daphne's eyes flitted to his for a moment. "Yeah. Sort of. Kind of on the downlow, though. Just waiting for Theresa to distract Morgan."

"We're... having a house meeting... without Morgan?"

The door to the armory suddenly burst open as an uncharacteristically flustered and disheveled Aaron stormed in. "Daph—"

"It'll be *fine!*" she said, refusing to meet his eyes.

"Which part?!" Aaron nearly shouted, waving his hands in the air. "The tight scheduling or the fact that I now have to get on stage wearing nothing but a tiny, sparkly bit of fabric over my junk?!"

Shane's eyes bulged, totally lost but wholly amused as he stared between the two of them.

"You did that to yourself," Daphne chuckled, shaking her head.

"I am *not* letting Morgan strip for a bunch of gooned up horn-dogs on Pleasure Avenue!" Aaron snapped, dropping into the seat at the head of the table.

"Out of concern for him or the horn-dogs?" Daphne snickered, deep in whatever she was doing on her comm.

"Yes," Aaron groaned. "I *know*... I know it's not fair. He's not happy about me doing it either. But this makes more sense. I can't break into the office like he can, and he's never... *performed* before."

"You have?" Shane interjected now that his ire seemed to be fading. "You've stripped?"

"For work," Aaron admitted, turning a bit red in the cheeks. "Undercover shit at Dickie Disco's. I was there for like a week."

"You at least get to keep the tips?" Shane asked, fighting back a grin.

"I *seriously* considered leaving my job and dancing full time," Aaron said with mild amusement. "Easiest rent month ever. And my abs looked *damn* good after moving like that for a few hours."

"We're here!" Gwen's voice echoed down the hall right before she peeked around the door, Lance hovering in the corridor behind her. "Oh, shit, Morgan's gone, right?"

"Yes," Aaron droned. "Frey, Percival, Gawain, get your asses in here!"

"My ass is already here," Frey grumbled from the chair across from Shane, giving him, Daphne and Aaron a start. "Grumpyface."

Aaron let out a heavy sigh. "Sorry... I'm so fucking nervous."

"Then let Morgan handle the stripping," Shane suggested, dropping into the chair beside Daphne, putting the same look of bewilderment he'd just shed on Gwen, Lance, Percival, and Gawain's faces as they shuffled inside.

"Why is Morgan stripping?" Gwen asked, glancing between the occupants of the table.

"He's not stripping!" Aaron half-shouted, looking completely exasperated. "I am. At Bloke's. In two days."

Gwen's fingers immediately leapt to her temples.

"No!" Aaron snapped, pressing his lips into a thin line with wide eyes.

"You don't know what I was doing!"

"You were checking your appointments to see if you had time to catch the show," Aaron growled, sinking back in his chair. "You're clear for the night, by the way. Already sorted."

Gwen's jaw fell as she swiped at her comm. "You meddled with my clients, but I'm not allowed to come watch you embarrass yourself?" She glared at Aaron. "I'm so confused."

"*I* meddled with your clients," Daphne admitted, tapping her fingers on the table. "You only had two, and they were both very understanding when I rescheduled them." She turned to Aaron, raising her brows. "Well?"

Aaron blew out a tight breath, shaking his head. "We're moving forward on our plans to infiltrate Esotech."

"By... showing the city your package?" Percy asked with a sheepish grin.

"Yes," Aaron said flatly. "No. I mean... shut up."

"Aaron is distracting the club," Daphne interjected. "Making sure all eyes are on him and that the place is packed. The city knows who he is now, thanks to the media, and it was either him or Morgan."

"Morgan... is breaking into the office of Lachlan Pierce, the owner," Aaron continued. "Daph got her lead. Pierce fumbled his way into a piece of Esotech's encryption code."

"Nice!" Shane shouted, leaning forward with a smile.

"No celebrating yet," Daphne said, shaking her head and hiding a grin. She spared Aaron a glance and a shrug. "Well, not on that front at least. It'll take some time to put the code to use. Once we know it's genuine, we'll put a plan together."

"Okay..." Lance shifted forward in his seat. "What do you need Gwen for?"

Daphne and Aaron locked eyes for a moment, then Daphne nodded encouragingly.

"I need you..." Aaron began, reaching into his pocket. "All of you." He fished a small black box out of his pocket, snapped open the lid, and spun it around on the table for everyone to see inside.

Shane merely glimpsed a glitter of silver, violet and blue before Gwen let out a shriek, clapping both hands over her mouth. "Oh my gods!" She leapt out of her chair, diving at Aaron to wrap him in a hug. "OH MY *GODS!*"

"It's so pretty..." Frey sang, mesmerized by the ring contained in the box—a sparkling trillion-cut stone wrapped in a silver band that resembled woven tree branches. "Is that... for Morgan?"

"You're proposing?!" Percival shouted, his face shining with joy as he jumped up next to throw himself on top of Gwen and Aaron. "Finally!"

"Finally!" Lance and Gawain echoed, sharing a laugh before they stood as well, clapping Aaron on the back.

Shane's cheeks hurt suddenly from an unstoppable smile. Aaron caught his eye beyond Gwen and Percival, grinning from ear to ear. With a laugh, Shane nodded. "I'm so happy for you guys."

"I don't get it," Frey muttered, glaring at the ring and rubbing their chest. "Why does the sparkly jewelry make everyone all warm and tingly inside?"

"Because it means," Daphne said softly, "Aaron and Morgan are getting married, sweetie."

"Oh…" Frey cocked their head, staring at Aaron as their eyes widened. "Oh! That's why Morgan's not here! It's a surprise! You're surprise marrying him? I don't think he'll like that."

"No!" Aaron laughed so hard he clutched his stomach. "I'm going to *ask* him to marry me, Frey. In two days, after our job."

"Stripping for a packed venue and then proposing to the love of your life?" Lance thumbed his lower lip, smirking at Aaron. "My, prenuptial customs have changed, haven't they?"

"Well, *you're* out as my witness," Aaron scoffed, returning his grin.

"Me?" Lance sputtered, taking a step back. "You want me to be your witness?"

Aaron shook his head with a befuddled laugh. "Of course I do, Lance; you're my best friend!"

"Hey!" Gwen punched him in the arm, pouting.

"What, you want to be my witness?"

"Maybe!" Gwen whined. She shrugged, then patted Lance on the chest. "No, you know what, I've done my time with these needy boys. Your turn."

"Thanks." Aaron rolled his eyes, snatching the ring off the table and tucking it back in his pocket.

"So, what do you need from us?" Percy asked, returning to his seat. "We're there. Whatever it is."

Nodding, Aaron leaned forward, glancing at everyone in turn. "I pulled some strings and got us a reservation at the Preluderian."

"Oooh!" Gwen squealed. "How did you manage that?"

"Calling in a *lot* of favors from my time with the force," Aaron sighed. "And little help from Daph."

"You're welcome." Daphne shot him a grin. "It's gonna be all hands on deck at the Maj. We're pulling out all the stops for the party afterwards."

"A party?!" Frey cheered, leaping from their chair. "I'm making clothes!"

"Yes!" Gwen pumped her fist, bouncing in her chair.

Aaron leaned forward with a soft shake of his head. "Morgan and I might not have time to change. I'm going to have him glamour something nice for us, just to be on the safe side."

"Fiiine..." Frey pouted, muttering under their breath, "I'm still making them..."

"All I want the lot of you to do," Aaron said sharply, "is help us make sure everything is ready to go and keep it under wraps. Do not even let Morgan *suspect* there is something to know. You know how he is."

"How long have you been planning for this?" Shane chimed in, knowing all too well they'd been at this for months at the very least. Daphne had told him on several occasions to mind his business, shooed him from the office more times than he could count, and caught plenty of shared glances between her and Aaron that indicated something was definitely up.

"Since Solstice," Aaron said with an airy laugh. "Daphne caught me researching the stone and *wouldn't let it go*."

"Again," Daphne sang, twirling her hand in a messy bow, "you're welcome. Had to get some outside help from another cipher to find that rock." She raised her brows at Aaron. "Should we invite Jazz to the party?"

"You two kept this from us for *six months?*" Gwen interrupted, her jaw hanging. "And you brought in a *stranger?*"

"You're not cursed anymore, princess," Aaron jabbed, folding his arms over his chest. "You seriously think you could've kept this from your gossip buddy that long?"

"Like hells," Lance mumbled under his breath, averting his eyes.

"You *hush*." Gwen slapped his thigh, wearing a fake scowl. "I'm still going to give him shit."

"Two days," Percy sighed, shaking his head. "We just have to keep it from Morgan for two days."

"I'll bind you all from breathing a word if I have to," Daphne offered. She leaned closer to Shane, grabbing his hands to lace their fingers together, making his heart flutter before she popped her eyes at him.

"W-What?" he sputtered. "I can keep a secret!"

"Pfft, okay," she snickered.

"I *can!*"

"Says the guy that told the entire OC that Morgan's an Ancient," Aaron chuckled.

"Hey!" Shane pointed a finger at him. "That never would've happened if your royal butt hadn't gotten kidnapped for a second time!"

"You *do* seem to get kidnapped a lot in this lifetime," Lance mused, arching a brow.

"You're right," Aaron sighed, waving a hand in the air. "S'all my fault. How dare I?"

"Totally a ploy," Gwen droned, shooting him a wink. "Had to play the prince in peril just to get Morgan to notice you."

"Whatever works," Aaron said with a shrug. His eyes turned sad as he heaved a sigh. "You know... I almost proposed before... before we all..." He swallowed, then met the eyes of his knights.

"Really?" Gwen breathed, reaching out to grab his hand.

Aaron nodded. "Morgan and I spent the night before we left the castle in our clearing. I could tell how worried he was for our ride east, but... I didn't know why. It was a peace envoy after all."

"He couldn't tell you, Aaron," Gwen said softly, a slight hitch in her voice. "You know he couldn't."

"I know," he sighed. "I came so close to saying the words... I had it all planned out—in our spot beneath the stars."

"Why didn't you?" Shane asked, searching his face.

"I couldn't," Aaron muttered, shaking his head. "I didn't know what was going through his head. He tried so hard to make that night special, and it was, but... he wasn't really there, you know? And I understood. I know how he gets lost in his own mind. But I feared the worst, and I didn't want him thinking I was only asking... because I was afraid that I might not get another chance."

The room stayed silent for a short time. Gwen took Lance's hand, still holding Aaron's in the other. Shane squeezed Daphne's hand, earning a sad smile in return.

It was strange sometimes, watching his friends grieve for their old lives. He wished more than anything that he could relate, that he could offer anything that might be a comfort to them. That he could repay them for all they'd given him and more.

"Aaron," Shane finally uttered. When Aaron met his eyes, he nodded. "He would've said yes then, and he's going to say yes now."

Aaron smiled in that dazzling way, making his eyes sparkle.

"You're getting *married!*" Gwen cooed, patting his arm.

"Alright, alright," Aaron laughed, swatting away Gwen's hand. "Morgan's gonna be back any minute. If he sees I've been crying, he'll never let it go until he makes the responsible party pay. Get out of here."

Everyone stood, giving hugs and patting Aaron on the back, offering congratulations again. As the knights left, Aaron turned back. "Hey, Shane?"

Shane raised his brows, moving closer.

"Look, I know how rough it's been on you these last few months, trying to get your magic going—"

"Nah," Shane droned, waving him off. "Don't worry about it, man. I'm good."

"Shane..."

"Okay, it sucks." It did. It really fucking did. But Shane never blamed his friends for that. Never would.

"I know," Aaron said softly. "I can't even imagine. And I want you to know that even with everything going on, we're still here for you. No matter how crazy shit gets, you know Morgan won't give up on you, and neither will I."

Shane drew a shaking breath, swiping at his eyes before tears could escape, nodding rapidly. "I know. I know that, man. I appreciate you saying it, though."

Aaron clapped him on the shoulder once with a smile, then turned to leave. Shane stared after him as he glided out into the hall, closing the door behind him.

Gods, the way he would give anything to get his magic working. All the tests they'd done, all the scans and research, only for him to create whirling balls of claws and furry rage with his runes. Every new lead they found broke something inside him a little more each time it led nowhere. Even now, Morgan was on the cusp of another potential breakthrough, but Shane didn't know how long he could keep hoping.

Sometimes he wondered if he'd be better off never having known, never having pulled that trigger.

But then he wouldn't have Aaron. He wouldn't have Morgan or maybe not even Daphne. He wouldn't have his family.

His home.

So, maybe... just maybe... he could make his peace with the magic already in his life.

A MAGIC TO BE RESTORED…

…A LOVE TO BE PROCLAIMED…

…A FATE TO BE BROKEN…

…AND A PATH—TO BE UNVEILED.

Acknowledgements

To those that stood by me when Atticus royally fucked me over right before releasing this book.

Jasmine and Keiri, for saving my butt with some workarounds.

Logan, Thea, and Mia for lifting me up and having my back.

The entire Rainbow Quill for letting me vent, making me laugh, and for being a shining example of what the MM Romance genre deserves. I want the world for each and every one of you.